A Matter of Possession

—a novel—

By L. Phillips Carlson

A Matter of Possession

—a novel—

By L. Phillips Carlson

© 2014 by L. Phillips Carlson

First edition

Published by

Snowsnake Press

PO Box 51732

Albuquerque NM 87181

Also available on Kindle and other devices

Printed by CreateSpace

Cover art and design by L. Phillips Carlson

Royalty-free butterfly clipart used with permission from

Microsoft

Acknowledgements

Thanks, as always, to the adept first-readers and critiquers whom I also count as good friends: Kathlena L. Contreras (K. Lynn Bay), Lara LaVonne Jordan, Lori Nicole Johnson and Wendy Bickel, all wonderful writers who have helped me so much.

And special thanks to my husband and family for their unflagging support. I couldn't do it without you!

Chapter 1

It was almost like Bea had staged the crappy weather to go along with her funeral. Joe Shurjack and his wife Teri crunched on the cold gravel paths between tombstones, heading toward the back of the cemetery where the open grave was. Little pings of sleet hit his umbrella, threatening to tear the fabric. Other semi-frozen blobs hit the nearby monuments, leaving marks like they'd been hit with clear-colored paintballs.

Joe half-smiled. Bea would have loved it.

An icy blast penetrated through his wool coat and his clothes underneath. He shivered. He hated the cold and wet. Teri, however, seemed unaffected by either the unusual spring storm or Bea Welford's untimely death. He couldn't blame her for the latter. Although he'd worked closely with Bea this past year, Teri had only met her once or twice in passing. And in spite of the slippery footing, Teri wobbled enough that he knew she'd imbibed her own type of antifreeze—a merlot perhaps—even though it was barely mid-morning. Unfortunately, that wasn't unusual.

The minister had already started the service by the time they reached the gravesite. No doubt he was just as eager as the rest of them to finish and go to a warm, dry home. Joe scanned the crowd—fifty or so, mixed ages and races, somewhat uncommon in still-segregated St. Louis but a testament to Bea's inclusive friendliness. Her family was nearest the casket: dark-skinned sisters and nieces and nephews, the ones she always bragged about. He also spotted Susan Fairchild and Chuck Amstead from the office, but didn't see their boss.

He sniffed. Also not unusual.

The group sang an out-of-tune rendition of "I Know That My Redeemer Lives." The traditional service right out of a Christian hymnal seemed inappropriate for Bea's larger-than-life persona, not to mention her own earthy attitude. She'd never even mentioned belonging to a church. Maybe the family had merely hired the minister for the day.

Another chill swirled around them.

The minister droned on with several prayers, then gave a short summary of Bea's life, making her sound like any middle-aged black woman, anywhere. Joe stared at his wet shoes. Where was the lusty joy of life she so embodied? The funny and pseudo-Southern pretense at manners? Where was the Bea he knew?

"Help us to receive your comfort as we remember and rejoice in Bea's life, cut short by a tragic car accident. We now place ourselves in your almighty hands and ask you to take away our sins—"

Sins. Joe winced inwardly and stole a sideways look at Teri. She seemed to be gazing off in the distance. He tried to quell his own sense of guilt. Two nights ago, he and Bea had gone out drinking after work, complaining about Donald Dressor, their boss and the biggest asshole private investigator in all of St. Louis County. It was easy to complain about him, the low wages and the boring jobs he gave them—ID and check fraud, cheating spouses. It was a wonder they hadn't been sent off to find lost dogs and cats.

They'd downed quite a few beers. Bea thought of herself as a cross between Mae West and Queen Latifa, buxom and teasing but a force to be reckoned with. She wasn't particularly pretty, but there was something Joe found quite appealing, nonetheless.

Too appealing, apparently. But he didn't remember what happened that night. At a late hour, he found himself in her apartment with a splitting headache and his pants around his neck, with her in a similar state of undress. He'd truthfully told Teri he'd tied one on, but didn't fill in the details, because he really didn't know.

Maybe he'd have to investigate himself, sorry ass that he was.

The service finally ended. As the funeral director started cranking the casket lower, Joe felt something like a cold hand slipping up his back and he shivered again. It was only the Missouri wind, but it seemed personal, somehow. How was it that Bea had been driving drunk? Sure, she liked her liquor, but he never remembered her getting behind the wheel inebriated. She had too many friends who could help out, plus the Red Bird Cab Company was number one on her phone contact list.

He turned to Teri, but she wasn't next to him anymore. Bea had often told him that he didn't pay enough attention and he hated to prove her right. Joe scanned the group quickly.

He finally spotted Teri kneeling near a corner of the grave's temporary tent, reaching for something. She drew back from the canvas folds as he approached.

"Look," she said. A small yellow butterfly quivered slightly as it clung to her glove. "Isn't that strange? A butterfly at this time of year?"

The poor thing looked as frozen as everyone else. "Yeah," Joe said. "Probably hatched in the storage room." It all seemed strange. Bea, gone. His dead-end job. His lousy marriage. Even the weather—no, actually, he had to admit it was pretty typical of St. Louis in spring. It merely sucked.

"Let's go home." He frowned. "You're not going to keep that thing, are you?"

Teri cocked her head to one side, very un-Teri-like. "Well, I just don't know, sugah."

Joe tensed. 'Sugah' was a pet name Bea liked to use for her friends. Was Teri mocking her? But how would she even know that nickname? Teri and Bea hardly knew each other.

He shook his head. "What did you say?"

Teri straightened rather abruptly and shook the insect off her hand. "I didn't say anything. What's wrong with you?"

He watched the butterfly fall to the icy ground and flop one wing as it died. "Never mind. Let's just get the hell out of here. Funerals just aren't my thing."

Teri cocked her head again. "Especially undeserved ones," she said with a slight drawl.

₭ℚ

The next morning was as gray as the day of the funeral. Joe battled his way through highway construction to the maze of one-way streets in downtown St. Louis. An anonymous jerk ignored a stop sign at one of the numerous three-way stops and nearly hit him. By the time Joe finally ended up in front of the old Coleridge Building, his favorite parking place had been taken.

Of course.

Shadows seemed deeper inside the office for some reason, while the Midwest late April sun lent a pale cast to Bea's empty desk. Someone had already cleared off the top, even down to the fake flower pens she liked to use. Maybe they'd cleaned out the drawers, he didn't know. There was something almost sacrilegious about that, like they were moving on too fast.

It wouldn't be easy without Bea. She handled a lot of the preliminary paperwork and background checks, along with organizing the office in general, and had even taken on some simple cases by herself. Today, a lot of her usual work was dumped in his office mailbox, except for the billing. Susan, their unreliable part-time office help, would be doing her unintentional best to foul that up all by herself.

He scooped up the stack of Dressor's scribbles and memos—"evidence," they said. But as he leafed through them, he noted headings for at least three different cases, all jumbled together. Sighing, Joe headed for the claustrophobic confines of his office and sat down to sort out the mess.

On top of his desk, right in the middle, was an envelope with his new PI license. Had he put it there? He didn't remember with the shock of Bea's death. He picked it up gingerly, as if it would burst into flame if he didn't treat it right. Maybe Teri would frame it for him. Or maybe not, when she learned that he got a full PI license, not just a renewal saying he was the employee of an investigative firm. Good old Missouri laws drew some curious distinctions in that regard. The difference in cost for a PI on his own was about ten times more—several hundred dollars. In addition, he'd have to get a business license, insurance, office space, furniture . . .

He stared at the certificate. What had he been thinking? He didn't have that kind of money.

"Got an invoice for you to check," a perky voice said.

Joe glanced at the open doorway. Susan's very pregnant belly preceded her, barely covered over with a tight T-shirt that said "Baby" with a downward arrow. *Duh*, he thought. It didn't take a newly-licensed investigator to figure that out. This was her—what, third?—and she always took ample time off whenever one of the kids was involved in something at school or as much as sniffled or coughed. He expected that she wouldn't be working here much longer.

Which left only him and Chuck to do all the evidence tracking and background checks and filing and phone calls—and—and—and—

Crap! he thought. Chuck was new and still learning the ropes, so he wouldn't be taking much more on. Joe might as well put on an apron and call himself a maid, because that's all he was going to do from now on, clean up Dressor's messes.

"Shurjack?" His boss's gravelly voice boomed from the outer office. "Where the hell's that evidence sheet for the Dunaway case? I gotta be in court in thirty minutes!"

Joe set down his certificate and hurriedly sifted through his desk's file drawer. "Got it—photos and the neighbor's affidavit that he really could work."

Dressor stood frowning in the doorway. "I hate insurance fraud cases. But it pays the bills." He snatched the papers out of Joe's hand.

Susan came to the door. "By the way, I need tomorrow afternoon off. I've got to run Jason to the doctor—"

"How do you expect me to run a business when nobody does a damn lick of work around here but me?" Dressor turned pink, starting with his ears. "No, you may not have that time off. Look, everyone cleared out yesterday for the funeral and I had to do everything myself. Damn inefficient use of my time." He spun around to face Joe. "That goes for you, too. With Bea gone, there's more work, so don't plan on taking time off in the near future."

Susan tugged at her T-shirt, a futile gesture to fully cover her baby bulge. Her dark eyes flashed. "You know," she said, her voice high-pitched, "my family comes first. My kids need me, and Jason needs to go to the doctor." She paused, a bit dramatically. "I'm giving my notice. I'm leaving tomorrow."

That wasn't a surprise to Joe. She was probably about to give birth, anyway.

Dressor tried to stare her down with those cold, shark eyes of his, but she stood her ground. *Rather like a mother bear,* Joe thought.

"Gather your shit and get out. I've tolerated your mistakes too long as it is." He raised his eyebrows and put on a fake smile. "Excuse me. Where are my manners? Have a nice life, Fairchild."

Susan sneered. "I intend to. And by the way, my maternity benefits don't run out until several months from now." She turned on her heel and headed for her office.

Dressor's ears were fully pink now. He turned to

Joe.

Joe felt his face grow hot. "What?"

"I was just thinking that maybe I should clean house." He grabbed a file from the stack on Joe's desk then slammed it back down. "This line of work requires a great deal of discretion, careful handling of both information and clients. Look at this mess! Bea didn't have what it took and I'm not sure you do either. Actually, I'm sure you don't have it. You've mishandled some of our files and cases."

"Mishandled? What the hell are you talking about?" Joe stood up. "I've never mishandled a case or the client's confidentiality!"

The older man raked his fingers through his comb-over. "Really? You worked with Bea on most of your cases, didn't you? I found all sorts of material last night that shouldn't have been in her desk."

"I didn't—I worked with her on some cases, not all. You're the one who assigned them, remember?"

"What about the Alder case, or Campolos?"

Joe tried to give an even-handed answer, but fire seemed to spit out of his mouth. "Those were Bea's. I've been working on Karstein. The only thing we've done together lately was the Dunaway case—the one you needed for court today."

Dressor's eyes pulled into a squint. Bea had said

he could've given Clint Eastwood serious competition with that look. "Is that so?"

"Yes, of course." Joe resisted an urge to punch something.

"Well." He started to leave, but turned back. "You're damn insubordinate in general, Shurjack. I simply can't have that. Get out."

"You're firing me?"

"I think you get the picture. You and Ms. Fairchild are free to go."

Joe couldn't think—what the hell just happened? "Just like that?"

Dressor nodded, eerily calm. "Just like that. Don't be here when I get back." He grabbed his hat and coat from a table in the outer office and abruptly left, the aged wooden door quivering in his wake.

"Whoa!" Susan slid out of her office. "Did he just flip or what?"

Joe fumed. After all the grunge, all the late nights working, all the missed time at home, this was his reward? And what the hell was all that about those files? The worst thing he'd done lately was pass a case involving family theft on to Bea—it was about a disputed butterfly collection, of all things! Such squabbles would likely have to be referred to a lawyer, since ownership within a family was a slippery thing. And likely, the lawyer wouldn't be able to do anything, either. Whoever had it, it was theirs now. Bea was always so good with irrational clients, and the three middle-aged sisters in this case really fit the bill. All Joe knew was it wasn't worth his or the agency's time.

He swore, good and loud, then saw the surprised look on Susan's face. "Sorry," he said, although he'd meant every word of it.

"That's all right," she said, "just let it out. I'd say it, too, but I've been trying to clean up my language around the kids."

Joe sat down hard and looked around. "Where did Bea's files go? They weren't in my mailbox."

She shrugged. "Maybe Chuck has them. He's not here right now. I think he went down to the police station in Creve Coeur, to talk to some guy in forensics."

"Yeah." Joe glanced at Chuck's desk in the corner. "He'll probably get moved into my office by tomorrow. Still, I don't get it. Why the hell would Dressor fire me? There's no way he can get all the work done with just Chuck left here. I'm mean he's learning, but—"

Susan smiled slightly. "But the nephew of Dressor's brother-in-law has some immunity from that sort of thing? Being fired, I mean. Or getting too much work dumped on him?"

Joe stared at his desk, not saying anything for a minute or two. Could he go to an employee advocate and force Dressor to change his mind? Did he even want to? It was all too weird, too soon after Bea's death. He glanced at the clock—it read 10:24, middle of the morning. It was going to be a very short work day, apparently. "I guess I better get my things together. This week started out really bad and it's certainly not getting any better."

Susan patted his hand in her mommy way. "To tell the truth, I already packed up, mostly. Could you help me in a few minutes? The box is a little heavy for me."

Joe carried her carton to the car and gave her a side hug. Maybe she hadn't been the best worker, but she always had a smile for him and knew what was going on in the office. She gave him a quick wave before she maneuvered her way into the driver's seat.

A sobering thought hit him. He'd never see Teri doing that funny pregnant waddle, unless she changed her mind about having kids. They'd only been married for five years, but it seemed like they should be thinking about kids, at least.

Of course, it'd be better if they had some income

other than Teri's part-time floor manager job at Felding's Department Store. He'd heard that the store was facing bankruptcy and in desperate negotiation for a merger. It wasn't surprising. Nobody shopped at old-time department stores anymore.

He stuffed his personal files into a briefcase, along with his laptop. What little he'd brought to the dingy office easily fit into a plastic crate and didn't take long to pack.

Joe took one last look. Two years of his life had been spent there, two grueling, crappy years of demeaning work. Oddly enough, he didn't feel badly about being fired. Maybe he should have quit a long time ago.

"You were right, Bea," he said to the air. "I need to start up my own firm. It's too bad you're not here. We could have done it up right."

A light in the back flickered. Joe's neck hairs quivered. He swiftly locked the door, shouldered his load, and didn't look back.

Chapter 2

It'd been all of a week since he'd been fired, but it felt like a lot longer. Joe popped a beer and sat down on the faded blue sofa in his living room. For days, he'd practically lived down at the unemployment office and the licensing bureau, trying to find some funds to tide him over until he could weave his way through all the red tape and get his own business up and running.

He took a swig, getting mostly foam.

On top of all that, Teri's hours got cut and here he was, without a job and with not much in the bank. He looked at the stack of bills on the end table. Their savings had taken a big hit when he went back to school to get his associates in Criminal Justice and never really recovered. He'd been doing his best to keep everyone happy, but some of those bills just weren't going to get paid. At least, not for a while. It seemed that every month, something happened to nearly wipe them out—a huge car repair, a blown water heater, a roof leak. It didn't take much.

Teri had been strangely quiet and wasn't drinking

as much as usual. Today she was off work and down at the shooting range with her brother, Ted. Joe sniffed. *Figures. I'm having a crisis and she's off having fun.* Although it wasn't his idea of fun. Her whole family belonged to the NRA, many of them competitors in matches held all around the country. Sober, Teri was a crack shot with any size pistol or a .22 lever action rifle. Even a little tipsy, she rarely missed.

The phone rang, and Joe grimaced. He'd already been hounded by one creditor and he didn't feel like talking to another. Now, without a job . . .

He rolled off the sofa and picked up the receiver gingerly. "Hello?"

"Um—wait a minute," a man's voice said.

Joe knit his brows. *What the hell?* He heard some papers being shuffled.

"Here it is." The voice was firm, but friendly. "Is Joseph R. Shurjack available?"

Joe paused a moment. "May I ask who's calling?"

"Joshua Baldridge, esquire. May I assume this is Mr. Shurjack?"

A lawyer. Damn, that probably meant a lien or something had been placed on him. "Yeah, it's me. What do you want?"

"A meeting, and it's rather urgent. Can you stop

by my office this afternoon, say, one- ish?"

"That depends," Joe said, "on whether it's gonna cost me money."

The man on the other end of the line laughed. "Oh, no, this one's pro bono. It'll be worth your time, I assure you. It concerns a letter from a mutual friend of ours, Bea Welford."

Joe stared at the phone. Bea didn't own much, so this wasn't a bequest or anything. The relatives at the funeral were saying they hoped to have enough to merely come out even on the estate. But he supposed he should check it out anyway. "What's the address?" he asked, and then wrote it down on a nearby scrap of paper.

Joe left a note for Teri. He hopped in his old Honda Civic and drove from Richmond Heights to the Central West End, the trendy neighborhood located just east of Forest Park and north of the huge Barnes-Jewish Hospital complex. New high-rise apartments threatened both the view and the rent levels, but the area reeked of gentility and quirky sophistication. Kitschy stores, high-priced restaurants offering fare from every continent, and, here and there, a dry cleaner or other service shop made up this small section of town. Just beyond the stores were old gracious homes, some invisibly divided into apartments, hiding behind massive iron gates that blocked entire streets.

And kept people like him from getting in.

Joe waited at a stoplight at Kingshighway and Lindell, staring at the huge limestone building before him. The venerable Chase Hotel still held court, so to speak, with its gilded lobby, movie theaters, bar and restaurant. "The Ghostbuster's Hotel," tourists called it, which the movie industry had mysteriously transplanted to New York City. Somehow, that always gave him a laugh. On a good day, the Chase looked more castle-like than foreboding, and today was a good day. Joe hoped that proved a good omen.

He dodged a few pedestrians leaving a sidewalk café. Joe fumed. *Why can't people pay more attention?* Finally, he stopped mid-block on Euclid Street, looking for the address he'd written down.

He double-checked the street number. This couldn't be right! It was a storefront with a blue and pink awning, most unusual for a lawyer. But he parked the car and walked back a half-block to take a closer look.

Joe pulled the glass door open and found himself in a small beauty shop. The only people there were a young, pink-uniformed woman and her client, a frumpy woman with streaked gray hair. The uniformed woman was vigorously applying lacquer to the other woman's nails.

Joe wondered if dark purple polish was "in" this year. He didn't know much about fashion, but to him, it made her nails look bruised.

The younger woman looked up and gave Joe a toothy smile. "Are you Mr. Shurjack? Josh is in his office, waiting for you." She tilted her head toward the rear of the shop, never stopping her work. "That way."

Joe thanked her and strode to the back, where a windowed door was left ajar. A hand-lettered sign taped to the frosted glass panel read, "Joshua Baldridge, LLD Attorney at Law."

Wow, Joe thought. *This guy's almost as bad off as I am.*

He knocked and entered, surprised to see a rumpled little man with dark hair, standing behind a very disorganized desk—with his back to him.

"Mr. Shurjack?" the man said, not turning around.

"Yes. Mr. Baldridge, I presume?"

The short lawyer finally turned around. "Quite right." He thrust a hand out, leaned over the messy desk and shook Joe's hand. "Sorry. Just checking my zipper. Hate to meet someone new with my fly down." He hurried around the desk. "Please, sit down." He then swept some notebooks off a chair with a smooth motion. "Here."

Joe wondered if he should use hand sanitizer when it was convenient. He sat, stiffly crossing his legs. "Uh, could you tell me what this is all about? I only put fifty cents in the meter."

Joshua Baldridge gave a good, deep laugh as he sat down behind the desk. "This won't take long. Sorry this place is in upheaval. My normal office is closer to the library, and it's being painted and fumigated and whatever else landlords like to do that interrupt business. Rosemary, my lovely fiancée, whom you've already met, is letting me use her office until I can get back into mine."

Joe leaned a bit forward. "I'm not so much concerned about the mess in here as the mess I might be in."

"Oh, no! You're not in any trouble. This is all about the letter." Joshua laughed again and dove into the left-hand stack on his desk, producing a tri-folded letter on elegant stationery. "From Bea."

Joe took a deep breath. "You may have heard that she passed away in a traffic accident last week."

The lawyer pressed his lips together and nodded, his unruly hair flopping over his eyes. "So sad. She was always the life of the party. We met at O'Toole's, down at Laclede's Landing. Very impressive woman. I understand she was a regular there." He flicked the hair out of his face and waved the letter. "She wrote a nice recommendation for you as a potential investigator for my firm. I can use a PI from time to time, and well, it's one of those times."

"Great—it so happens I'm looking to pick up more cases." Joe smiled, trying not to look desperate.

Joshua continued. "I've got the weirdest case. Involves butterflies, if you can believe that."

"Yeah," Joe said, his heart sinking. "That's probably the case I turned down at the PI's office where Bea and I worked."

"You turned it down?" Joshua asked, his wooly eyebrows rising in almost comic surprise. "Really? Why?"

Joe shrugged. "It was a family dispute over a collection. In fact, I asked Bea to refer them to a lawyer."

"Ah, and here they called me. I suspect that Bea must have had a hand in that. But this case—oh, you'll like this! It's gotten much more complicated than a familial theft."

Joe was all ears.

Joshua's face lit up and he tapped his fingers on

the desk. "The disputed collection was in the possession of a woman named Ramina Burl, much to her two sisters' chagrin. It was an heirloom collection and they all felt they should have a piece of it. Then it really did get stolen—not by a family member but by some thief. And, most unfortunately, one of the younger sisters had threatened Ramina. As of this morning, Ramina Burl turned up dead—shot once, in the chest."

"Sounds like a family squabble turned ugly."

Joshua shook his head and continued. "Cecile—that's the sister who threatened Ms. Burl—called me shortly after she was arrested and has retained me as her lawyer. After talking to her, I have a gut feeling that she didn't do it."

"And you need proof."

He shrugged. "One way or the other. I don't like losing cases and don't want to take it to court unless I'm sure where I stand. So whatever you find out is fine by me. By the way, she's got plenty of money and will pay expenses. You in?"

Joe thought quickly. He'd have his business up and running in a matter of days, but he lacked cash to subscribe to some of the data services he'd be using. "You bet! But I'll need a retainer to get started."

"Um? OK." Joshua absent-mindedly scribbled a

number on a piece of paper. "These are my standard rates."

"Oh." Joe tried not to overreact to all the zeroes. "I think that'll be just fine. Plus travel and hotel, if needed," he added, trying to look professional.

"I'm sure that can be arranged."

Joe stuck out his hand. "You got a deal, then. Butterflies it is."

Joshua gave him a vigorous handshake. "Great! Rosemary has a copy of Cecile's deposition and some contact numbers. I suggest starting with the third sister, Meris. She's due back in town tomorrow. Some ski trip to Colorado, I think."

Rosemary stuck her head in the doorway. "I'm supposed to remind you to get to court."

"Thanks, love. We're just finishing up." He looked at Joe. "Anything else?"

Joe smiled and shook his head. His first solo case!

Joshua gathered a few dog-eared papers and stuffed them into a worn leather case. "If you've got any questions, feel free to call. I don't charge my contractors or employees for phone time." He smiled broadly. "That's a little lawyer humor."

Joe nodded and smiled back. With what Joshua was paying him, he could use whatever kind of humor he wanted.

He waited in the office alone while Rosemary hunted up the requested documents along with some papers to establish him as a contractor for the firm. He glanced down at Bea's letter, which Joshua had left folded on top of one of the paper stacks. He opened it, curious as to what she had said about him.

It was handwritten and gave a glowing account of his abilities. He hoped he could live up to the image she'd painted of him. *What a great gal,* he thought.

As he started to replace the letter, he noted the date—April 21, a day *after* she'd died.

What the hell?

Shaking, he also noticed the particular design of the black and gold-edged stationery. It looked exactly like—like—

—like Teri's formal correspondence.

Rosemary appeared with a couple of folders and frowned. "You need some water or something?" she asked. "You look a little pale."

Joe slid a little lower in his seat. "Yeah, thanks. I'm feeling a little sick."

Real sick, actually.

Chapter 3

Joe drove into his garage and turned off the ignition.

Bea was dead. He'd seen her body at the wake, gone to her funeral. So how had that letter shown up at the lawyer's, dated a day later?

Of course! He closed his eyes for a moment. She must have made a mistake on the date. Lots of people do that.

But—he tapped his wedding ring on the steering wheel—it looked like Teri's stationery. He took his hands off the wheel. Dummy, he told himself. Lots of people buy the same stationery. It's not like it was terribly unique. Every Hallmark store in the country probably had a half-dozen boxes of that particular design.

And yet—Bea's taste was usually more flamboyant than the simple designs that Teri favored.

Something in his gut told him things weren't quite right, and it wasn't the bratwurst he had for lunch, either. He grabbed his gear and went into the house.

Teri was leaning over the kitchen counter, staring at a folded newspaper. Her butt stuck out, which struck him as odd, since she was rather skinny in that department, so the effort looked forced. Bea used to stand that way, he reminded himself, but her curvy shape made it look easy.

"Hi honey," he said, hoping to rouse her out of whatever she was engrossed in.

She jerked upright and turned slowly toward him. A wide smile formed on her face. "Hey, doll. Just reading about my demise. Care to see?"

"What are you talking about? Are you feeling sick or something?"

She moved an arm stiffly. "I'm just fine, sugah. I'm still getting used to this body—a bit underfed, if you ask me. She must only eat crap like celery and bean sprouts to look like this."

Joe's neck prickled. "Teri, this isn't funny at all. What the heck is wrong with you?"

A very Bea-like condescension flickered across her face. "Nothing, except this isn't Teri. It's me—Bea. I've just borrowed Teri's body for a spell."

He took a big step back. "Look, I know Bea's death affected you—it affected both of us, but this isn't the way to deal with it."

She fixed him with a stare. "Like you dealing with

our night out last week?"

Beads of sweat formed on his brow. How did Teri learn about that? "I don't know what you're talking about—" he started, feeling weak.

She waved a hand. "Oh, relax, she doesn't know anything about it. I'm certainly not going to tell her that you ended up half-dressed in my bed. I'm not going to tell her anything, about us, about our cases—" she stopped. "Oh, I see! You want me to prove this, don't you?" She pursed her lips and folded her arms in front of her. "Ever the dick, aren't you?"

He grabbed a chair by the table and sat down. "OK, if you're really Bea—and I don't believe in ghosts, by the way—tell me what case you told your lawyer friend about, the one you recommended me for?"

She put a finger on her jaw and looked skyward, very coy. "The now-deceased Ramina Burl case, involving some missing butterflies belonging to her father, I believe, and two very jealous sisters."

Joe sat there, his face frozen. "Bea? That really is you!"

"That's what I've been tryin' to tell you, sugah." She sighed. "Men! You can be so dense." She shivered and seemed to lose her balance, catching herself on the counter. "Look, I don't have much time. I haven't quite got this possession thing down—and Teri's fighting to come back."

Joe blinked a few times. "Where is she? Is she OK?"

"Just shut up—please? I have to get this out." Bea took a huge breath, one that would have made Teri hyperventilate if she'd done it. "Joe, you gotta help me! I didn't die naturally. I wasn't even drunk. I was tired that night and headed straight home."

"What about the alcohol the cops found?"

She waved a dismissive hand. "I bought a bottle of wine—to drink later—and it broke in the crash. Listen, do you think I'd be stupid enough to drink and then drive 65 miles an hour on the 64/40? At rush hour?"

Joe raised his eyebrows. "So, what happened?"

"That's what I'd like to know." She drummed her fingers on the counter. "My car needs to be looked at. I think it was tampered with."

"But why? And who—"

Bea shook harder, like she was cold. And then it was Teri—Joe could tell by her sad eyes and the little downturns on the sides of her mouth. She looked at him like she'd just woken up.

She frowned. "When did you get home? I didn't even hear you come in."

Joe swallowed hard, unsure of what to say. "Uh, just a few minutes ago. I didn't want to disturb you. You seemed involved with something or other."

Teri picked up the newspaper from the counter and handed it to him. "Yeah, I saw this article about Bea and the dangers of drunk driving. Not very complimentary." She shrugged, a cute little one-shoulder twitch that was so typically her. "So, how did it go with the lawyer? I found your note."

"Oh!" Joe was more than happy to change subjects. "Got a job—temporary one, but it'll pay well."

"Great." She frowned again and didn't seem to be listening.

"Teri?"

She put a hand to her forehead. "I suddenly have this headache. I'm going to have to lie down." She left for the living room without saying another word. Soon, Joe heard the TV come on, some reality show.

Joe sat at the table, not moving for several minutes, not able to think. If he'd been any kind of a decent PI, he should've been trying to process what just happened.

Which was—he'd been talking to a freakin' ghost. In the middle of the day, in his kitchen. Like it was all normal. Except that it wasn't.

And what if it were true—that Bea's car was tampered with? Who would do that and why? How could anyone dislike someone like Bea—at least, enough to kill her?

He got up and poured a big glass of red wine. Maybe he'd have to start believing in the paranormal now.

He took a generous gulp of wine, and then held the glass out.

Here's to you, Bea, he said in a silent toast. *I'll check it out, anyway.*

Chapter 4

From all appearances, Meris Burl was a flake. Correct that, Joe said to himself, a rich flake. The stocky woman in her thirties hadn't bothered to comb her dyed-blonde hair or remove last night's make-up for their interview. He was also pretty sure that pearls with a mismatched sweat suit hadn't made the fashion tabloids.

And there was an unmistakable odor of gin.

"Regis!" she barked.

The butler who had shown Joe into the Burl mansion reappeared inside the heavily-draped study and patiently waited for his orders.

"Have Cook send up some coffee and scones. Tell her strong coffee." After the butler left, Meris gave a practiced smile and waved at a chair. "Sit down, Mr.—sorry, I forgot your name."

"Shurjack. Call me Joe." He sat in an overstuffed wing chair.

"From Cecile's lawyer's office, right?"

"Yes. I have a few questions for you."

She nodded and looked around the room. "Well, I

guess it makes sense to talk to me since I'm now in charge here, with Ramina gone and Cecile in jail. I mean, I even had to leave Durango early for this. And the spring snow's really good this year." She sighed. "Duty first."

Joe raised his eyebrows. "Cecile bonded out yesterday. I thought she might be staying here with you."

"She's out already?" Meris snorted. "No, she's not here. Cecile hates the family home. She rarely comes to visit. I never come here either, until now, that is. It was Ramina's place, she made that very clear to the rest of us."

A young woman entered the room, carrying a polished ebony tray with coffee, tea, and pastries on it. "Will there be anything else, ma'am?"

"Yes," Meris said, with a dismissive wave. "I'd like to be left alone."

The girl bobbed her head, then tugged at the study's sliding double doors and pulled them shut from the outside.

"Now," Meris said, heaping spoonfuls of sugar in a cup and adding what little coffee would fit, "why are you here again?"

Joe half-expected her to offer him something to eat or drink from the ample spread before her—which he would have refused, since he was working—but the offer didn't come. He cleared his throat. "As you may know, Cecile has retained Joshua Baldridge as her attorney, and I'm here to gather what information I can that would help her."

"You want information on Cecile? Well, she's a greedy bitch, for starters," Meris said, rubbing her already smeared mascara. "If she hadn't complained so much about the stupid butterflies, we all wouldn't be in this mess."

Joe pulled out a notepad from his briefcase. "What do you mean?"

"I mean, who wants a bunch of dead insects on your wall, anyway? Yeah, they were worth some money, but they were hardly worth the life of our dear sister, Ramina." Meris' voice dripped with almost as much sugar as she'd put in her coffee. "But Cecile, she always worried about her fair share. She's been hassling the family trust officer ever since Daddy died, trying to get more than what she's due. We're all on an allowance, you know. I mean, it's juvenile, like we can't be trusted with what's really ours."

"May I ask how much that is?"

"The allowance?" Meris' eyes narrowed. "I suppose I can tell you—your lawyer friend has ways of finding out, anyway, I'm sure. It's not a huge amount—about $20 million a year."

Just a pittance. Joe made a note of the amount in his binder. "For each of you?"

A look of disgust came over her. "No, for the three of us to share. That's not considered much in the circles I run in." She took a swig of coffee. "Share and share alike. That's what family is for." She took a big bite of pastry, swallowed, then brightened. "Although, I guess that'll be changing now that Ramina's gone." She looked around the room as if inventorying the valuables, then sighed. "I suppose I'll have to go through her stuff soon and decide what to keep. She never married, no kids. Cecile and I are it as far as family goes."

Joe scribbled down some more notes. Such tender, loving thoughts for the dearly departed. "So, tell me what you know about the night before last."

Meris shrugged. "I wasn't here—I was in Purgatory."

"Pardon?"

"It's a ski resort in southwestern Colorado. I met up with a half-dozen friends. They can all tell you."

"I'm sure they can, Ms. Burl. I was wondering what you know about what happened here during the robbery."

Meris turned in her chair, the morning light

catching her face. She had considerably more wrinkles than most people her age, like she'd spent too much time between taverns and the outdoors. She shrugged. "Somebody broke in and stole Daddy's bugs. Nothing else was taken—not even Ramina's Rolex, which she had forgotten in the billiards room—it was right on the pool table, I was told. I guess she surprised the robber and he shot her. Or else it was planned, I don't know. I wouldn't put it past Cecile to have hired the whole scene."

Joe put his pen down. "It doesn't sound like you and your sisters are very close."

Meris looked at him and laughed. "It doesn't take much of a detective to figure that out, Mr. Shurjack."

He smiled grimly. No, it didn't, and he wasn't getting anywhere with this interview.

After getting phone numbers for her friends, he thanked her for her time. Soon he was again in the company of Regis, the butler. None of the staff was on duty the night of the break-in, leaving Ramina alone in the turn-of-the-century mansion. The police had already questioned them and they all had tight alibis, but he'd double-check the official report when he got it. Joe glanced around the house as the butler showed him through. Marble floors, oil paintings, niches with bronze statues, expensive everything. Old, old money—fancy now, unimaginable riches back in the late 1800s when the house was built. Finally, they reached the billiards room, festooned with suburban University City police yellow tape, labeling it as a crime scene.

It wasn't a tidy place. The dark-paneled room had a stale smell like it'd been closed up for some time. Dust coated every piece of the carved, walnut side tables and chairs that ringed the custom-built pool table. Joe trod gingerly around the scene, careful not to touch anything. He took a few photos with a pocket camera—the bloodstain on the floor where Ramina fell, a broken vase by the wall, the empty spaces on the sun-faded panels where the butterflies had been. The intruder had apparently broken in via a stained-glass door in a small anteroom that led to a vine-covered terrace in back. Shards scattered over the threshold, like a broken kaleidoscope.

Joe noted the dusty floor in the hall by the anteroom, too, and snapped a picture. As his camera flashed, dark spots came to life on the terrazzo tile. He frowned. Footprints? He wondered if they'd been marked as evidence.

He pulled out a penlight and saw several prints from a man's shoes, both going from the anteroom and then heading back to the crime scene. Maybe it was nothing, but he carefully placed his penlight by one print for scale, then snapped another picture.

Back in his car, Joe called in an official request for copies of the police photos and report, to be sent to Joshua since he was Cecile's lawyer. He also gave his own information to the desk sergeant who answered the phone, and then made a note of the detective in charge.

Joe sat in his car for a while, thinking. Judging from his own feet, those shoeprints in the hall were about a size 12. The butler had small feet, and the rest of the staff were women. The hall was beyond the yellow tape. Had the police missed that? If so, he would certainly need to talk to them about it.

Joe started his car and drove out of the Burl's neighborhood, past other old, gracious homes, all considerably more than he could afford—at least in this lifetime. He turned onto Delmar Street. In the summer, trees along this portion of the street formed a leafy canopy. Now, though, the bare, black limbs, not quite budded out, stood like a broken fence of unfriendly sentries.

By the time he reached the towering Lion Gates at the suburb's boundary, the light turned red, forcing him to wait. He stared at the two columns flanking the road. Few knew the noble beasts on top were plastic replacements for the original marble lions, which were too heavy for the columns to support.

They were fakes, just like the so-called upper crust Burl family.

He shook his head. Three siblings who all hated each other. He'd been an only child, and his parents had died young with a lot of debts. It'd be nice to have some family around, someone who could back you. He only had Teri.

If Teri was still Teri, that is. Joe gritted his teeth and sped home, wondering who would be in her body this time.

ഇരുൽ

His wife—or the woman who looked like his wife—was on the phone in the den, cradling the receiver between one shoulder and cheek while holding a notepad and scribbling.

Left-handed.

Damn it, Joe thought. Teri was right-handed.

"Hello," he called out, gingerly.

Teri/Bea hung up the phone. "About time you got here. You said you were going to help me."

"I haven't forgotten," Joe said. He set down the backpack he used as a briefcase. "I had to interview one of the Burl sisters and check out the crime scene for the butterfly/murder case."

She sniffed. "You should have let me know. I could have come along as your wingman."

OK, it was definitely Bea. Teri never used words like "wingman."

"Yeah, and how am I supposed to call you out? Teri was here when I left." Joe plopped on the worn sofa. "I'm sorry, this is just too weird—you being dead and all."

"Tell me about it. I'm still getting used to it myself." Bea curled into an arm chair. "But it's real, believe me, sugah. It's as real as the other night."

"I don't suppose you're going to tell me about that?" Joe unclenched his hands, suddenly aware that he'd locked them together.

She gave a sly smile. "When the time's right."

He looked down and noted opened letters on the coffee table. "What the hell? Have you been going through my mail?"

"Yes," Bea said, matter-of-factly. "I take it you didn't get very far with what's her name? Meris?"

Joe frowned. "Don't change the subject. I don't like the idea of you going through my mail."

"But you didn't get much info, did you, sugah?" She put on a Cheshire Cat grin.

He spread his hands in surrender. "No, I didn't.

What do you suggest, Miss Omnipotent Ghost?"

"I wish! About the omnipotence, I mean." Bea shrugged. "If it were me, I'd contact the ALCA—the American Lepidoptera Collectors Association, and ask if any unusual specimens have come up for sale lately. You did get exactly what was stolen, didn't you?"

Joe stared at her. Damn! She always let him know where he'd messed up. "I was concentrating on the dead person, not the dead bugs."

Bea pursed her lips. "Darlin', I looked it up on the web. Some of those dead bugs go for several G's apiece. Historic ones—sixty, seventy years old, or ones from weird places in Africa and South America."

Joe thought for a moment. "Meris didn't seem to know much about anything other than partying. I need to talk with the accused sister, Cecile. Maybe she can get me insurance records or some photos of the room when the butterflies were still in there."

"Now we're thinkin'," Bea said, jiggling Teri's small bosom. "And now, to the real business?"

Joe ignored her come-on and pulled out one piece of official-looking mail. "Is this the police report of your accident?"

Bea nodded.

"I assume you ordered it in my name?" What else had she been up to? He glanced at her sternly. "Did it say anything?"

"No." Bea spat out the word. "Not one dang thing. Said I was probably intoxicated and ran my car into a retaining wall. They didn't include the actual car inspection. I don't even know where the damn car is."

Joe looked it over. "There's a reference to the mechanic who inspected the vehicle. Apparently it was contracted out by the police department to someone named Pete Smitters."

"Smitters?" Bea tilted her head and waved a finger. "I know that name! Dressor used him on some stolen auto cases that came through the agency. And I remember Smitters Automotive being in accounts payable from time to time." She looked at Joe with wide eyes. "He's got to be lying about this! You gotta believe me—I pushed the brake pedal and nothing happened!"

"OK, don't get excited here. I'll talk to him and get you some answers."

"When?" Bea asked then shuddered violently.

"Tomorrow, maybe. Probably."

She squinted, like she'd just woken up. "What about tomorrow?" she asked in a thin voice. "And when did you get home? I didn't hear you sneak in."

Whoa. Change gears. Joe smiled slightly. "Teri. I

thought you looked tired. So I said why not cook dinner *tomorrow*. We could order out a pizza tonight." He quickly shuffled his papers together.

"Works for me." Teri frowned and looked around the den. "I—I guess I fell asleep or something. What time is it?"

"Almost noon."

"Really?" She checked her watch. "I've got a one-o'clock appointment for a part-time job at one of the dress shops in the Galleria. I need to get going." She started to leave, then turned back to face him. "Didn't you tell me you had to meet some woman for that case you're working on?"

"Already did earlier today. Didn't get much."

Teri did her one-shoulder shrug. "Oh well, I'm sure you'll find something soon. You always do." She waved and headed up the stairs.

Joe wasn't sure she was being positive or blasé. It was always so hard to tell with her.

He returned to his stack of letters and saw Bea's notepad on the end table. He shouldn't leave such evidence around for Teri to find. He snatched up the pad and noted the distinctive handwriting, same as on the note she'd sent to Joshua Baldridge.

He shook his head. Just something else to keep track of.

Chapter 5

Joe wiped his feet on the dirty welcome mat in the small automotive shop, vainly trying to remove whatever grease he'd just stepped in. A mechanic bent under the hood of a pale green Ford Fusion. "Hello?" Joe called.

The young man pulled out slowly. "Customers 'sposed to wait in the other room," he gestured with a wrench.

Joe ignored him. "I'm looking for Pete Smitters."

The man regarded him for a moment, then turned back to his work. "He's in the pit by the far bay."

"Thanks." Joe walked over quickly before someone else told him to leave. The bay looked abandoned—just an old Toyota with a small light under it—until he heard some swearing underneath and then a clunk. He half-smiled. That was the way Joe's dad had always "coaxed" things to fit. It made for a lot of dents and problems later.

"Hello?" he called again. "Pete Smitters?"

A gangly man of about forty emerged from the pit. "I'm him. This better be important, I got a whole parking lot of cars to work on today." He wiped his hands on a pocket rag.

"Joe Shurjack. I'm doing some follow-up on the Welford car for Northland Insurance. You inspected it last week for the Clayton police department?"

"Welford? What kind of car was it?"

"'04 Malibu hatchback. Dark red."

Pete took a deep breath. "You guys are supposed to make appointments. This is real inconvenient."

"It won't take long," Joe said.

The grimy mechanic looked heavenward and then frowned. "Fine. I'll give you five minutes, but you tell your people that I'm pissed about it. I'm doing you a favor to stop work and all." He stomped off toward a small back office, Joe following.

Pete switched on the light and booted up his computer. After swearing at its slow speed, he finally pulled up the right page. "Here it is. Apparently the driver was drunk as a skunk. Car's a helluva mess now."

"The driver died," Joe said softly.

"Not surprised." Pete whistled through his teeth. "What's left of the car is at Dugham's Salvage in Florissant. I'll print this out so you have a copy." He tapped a key. "Anything else?"

At least he found out where the car was. Joe

scanned the document. Could Bea have been mistaken about the drunk part? She'd been so adamant. Yet there was nothing on the report to indicate mechanical failure. "No, I think that's about it. Can I call you if I have questions?"

Pete raised one side of his lip. "Make an appointment next time. We're workin' people here, the hands-on kind, not a bunch of pencil-pushers. Had to let a guy go last week and it's been extra busy." He walked out of the office and held the door, making it obvious that Joe was to leave, too.

"Thanks," Joe said. Something in his gut said things weren't quite right. He looked around for a distraction. "Say, is there a men's room around here?"

Pete took a deep breath, then dropped his shoulders as he let it out. "Through the waiting room, over there." He waved a greasy rag and went back toward the Toyota, muttering.

Joe entered the dingy waiting room and made his way around worn, plastic chairs. He stopped in front of the restroom door and turned around. Through a transverse window that separated the room from the garage, he could see that Pete had disappeared into the last bay. He waited a few more moments, then ducked back into the work area.

"Hey," he said to the first mechanic. "I was

looking for a guy who worked on my car last week, but I guess he doesn't work here anymore. What's his name?"

"Hector?" The young man looked blankly at him. "Gonzales?"

"Yeah, that's him," Joe said. "Do you know where I can get hold of him? He did real good work."

The mechanic sniffed. "That's not what the boss said." He looked around quickly. "Look, I gotta get back to work. I think Hector lived off Arsenal, near downtown, if that helps."

"Thanks. If I don't find him, maybe I'll bring my car to you. You look like you know what you're doing."

The man gave a grim smile. "Yeah, don't be too long about it. I may be working somewhere else by then, too."

Back in his own car, Joe took out his cellphone and started an address search. There were several matches with such a common name, but luckily, a few phone calls later, he found the right Hector and convinced him that they should meet.

He pulled up to an old brick fourplex, just a short way south of the Arch, in an area badly needing renovation. A dark-haired Hispanic man with a can of chew watched him from a folding chair in the trash-strewn front yard.

Joe suddenly wished he carried a firearm. Not that he was any good at using it, but it would have made him feel better just to have it.

He introduced himself and stuck out his hand.

Hector just eyed him. "Who'd you say you work for?"

"Northland Insurance." Joe was glad he'd asked Bea for that info. "We're investigating an accident that happened last week."

Hector didn't say anything.

"I'm not sure you were the one who inspected Ms. Welford's car last week—the '04 Malibu hatchback—but maybe you can remember something about Mr. Smitters—"

"He's a crook." Hector spat his mouthful of chew onto the ground, then took another. "He's a big, goddamn crook. He owes me two weeks wages, too."

Joe cleared his throat. "There is a question about the accuracy of the report sent to the police—"

Hector laughed. "Yeah, I'm sure about that. He never looks at 'em. Just takes the money and signs 'em."

"And Ms. Welford's car—"

"Like the rest." Hector spat again and stood up.

Joe took a step back, not sure what to expect.

"Look, I don't know nothing." He scowled, then kicked the chair he'd been sitting in. "Maybe you better ask that *mujer* who came into the garage. She probably knows something. She and that piece of *caca* ex-boss of mine talked, then I saw money go from her hands to his."

"Did you hear what they said?"

Hector snorted. "Like I care. I think that's what got me fired—being too close to them. I told him I didn't hear nothing, but he didn't listen. And now, how am I gonna pay for my place and my woman?" He extended a hand, palm up.

Joe took the hint and pulled out his wallet. "All I got is a couple fifties."

Hector grabbed the bills. "It'll do. Don't use my name, amigo. I'll deny it all."

"Agreed. Did you see what the woman looked like?"

"Dark hair, a white woman. Really pale. One of those women who used to look real good and now uses too much make-up, you know the type? They try too hard to look younger."

Joe nodded. "I hate to ask, but are you sure she wasn't just a customer paying her bill?"

Hector gave him a menacing look and made a fist by his side. "I signed 'em all in. She weren't no customer. And she mentioned the Malibu."

"Aha. Anything else? Identifying marks, that kind of thing?"

"Yeah. She had a tat on her hand. I thought it was a big mole or something, but it was a tat, right here." Hector pointed to the back of his hand. "It was red. A strawberry, I think."

"Right or left hand?" Joe asked.

Hector shrugged. "Don't remember. All I know is she came in asking about the Malibu, and then she gives Smitters money and she leaves."

"Look, if you remember anything else about this, give me a call, OK?" Joe dove into his pocket and pulled out a newly-printed business card.

"Sure," Hector said, tossing the card into the lawn. "No problem."

೫⋈೪

Joe finished reciting what he'd learned and closed his notebook. "Do you have any idea who this mystery woman could be?"

"Boy, would I like to get hold of that gal." Bea rubbed her hands together. "But I don't think I know anybody like that, especially with a tattoo on her hand. Now if you'd said it was on the breast or butt, I could name quite a few folks." She shifted on the sofa.

"I don't like it, Joe. Some stranger and an exchange of money—about my car, too! Something's wrong. I can feel it."

Joe had to agree. "Maybe a look at the car will give us some answers."

Bea nodded. "I know a mechanic who could go up to Dugham's and check it out. He's a good guy and would probably do it for free. You'll have to call, though. I don't think he'll believe it's a request coming from me."

He smiled. "Probably not. Write down the name and I'll call this afternoon. And, at some point soon, we need to discuss what cases you were working on and who else was involved—clients, police, whoever."

She shrugged. "Dressor gave me all of them, so they should be logged in at the agency. They weren't much—mostly insurance cases, and he decided I wasn't good enough to do even those. The asshole took most of them back to do himself. I'm glad you're not working for him anymore."

"Me, too. Have to say the steady income was nice, but it wasn't worth the degradation."

Bea rose off the sofa and sidled next to his chair. "Joe, sugah, you just don't know what this means to me." Before he could respond, she planted a kiss on his cheek—not a friendly peck, but a lingering kiss. At least, as much as Teri's thin lips could do.

"Bea," Joe said, then cleared his throat, "when are you going to tell me about that night we went drinking together? Sometimes I think you like torturing me."

She smiled slyly. "Teri's got another appointment at the mall dress store. Gotta go get ready." She sashayed out of the room, making the most of Teri's slim hips.

Joe stared at the doorway. *Women.* He'd never understand either of them.

Chapter 6

Another day, another lead going nowhere.

"So," Joe said to Cecile Burl, trying to probe her for something beyond the exasperating politeness she displayed, "do you have any idea what kind of butterflies were stolen? I understand that some kinds of butterflies and moths—the old or foreign ones—can be very valuable."

Cecile tipped her head to one side in a practiced pose. The small woman in front of him seemed so different from her bawdy sister—thin, brown-haired, and refined. Except for a similar nose and chin, it would be hard to peg the two as siblings.

And her home was as restrained as she was—mostly decorated in beiges and neutrals, carefully accented here and there with a subtle maroon pillow or a dark blue lamp. They sat in her living room, a rather modest affair compared to the regal Burl mansion now occupied by Meris, although the first quality furniture and some of the knick-knacks—porcelain figurines, silver candlesticks and the like—showed the money she likely sat on.

"I'm sorry, I don't have the exact inventory, but I think it was insured with Homecrest. Daddy always did business with Homecrest. I can call and find out for you, if you wish."

"That would be most helpful." Joe jotted down the name of the insurance company.

"Daddy's collection was mostly from North and South America and had many kinds," she said, counting on long, elegant fingers. "Swallowtails, metalmarks, gossimerwings, brushfoots, skippers—he had them all. Some he caught himself on repeated trips to Mexico, but mostly he bought older specimens. He did have a few from other places, too. I do remember that Daddy's pride and joy was a male butterfly from New Guinea, the largest kind in the world: a Queen Alexandra's Birdwing. It was truly beautiful—shimmery blues and greens and a yellow belly—and huge—as big as my father's hand span. It was old and he didn't display it often, afraid it would fade in daylight. Did you know that it's illegal to collect them now? It was a perfect specimen, too, virtually priceless."

Joe tapped his pencil. "It sounds like you're fairly knowledgeable about butterflies yourself."

She shrugged and spread her hands slightly, another apparently practiced move. "It was a way to spend time with Daddy. He loved his collections and rarely talked about anything else." She removed her glasses and laid them in her lap. "I should say he loved the common butterflies and moths, too—the monarchs and sulfurs and Cecropia moths that you find in every field around here. He just loved all their colors, shapes and sizes. An insatiable collector. Besides the ones displayed on the wall, he had drawers full of framed specimens up in his bedroom."

Joe frowned. Neither the police report nor Meris had said anything about that. "And what happened to those?"

Cecile grimaced. "All gone. Everything was stolen. It's like his life work meant nothing."

Joe made a note to return to the mansion and check it out. Why had this been missed? Seemed like a huge flaw by the crime scene team. Like him, they were probably too focused on the dead body in the room.

He also wondered if he was being too much like a cop to get good responses. He set his notepad down in an attempt to be more conversational. "Was Ramina involved with the collection as well?"

Cecile seemed to come out of a reverie. "Oh, no. Like Meris, she hated insects. She was always the independent one, the one with good business sense. I think that's why Daddy left her in charge of house and the estate." She shrugged again. "I didn't always agree with her decisions, as you know from my deposition. I assume you've read it?"

Joe nodded. Actually, he had.

"Ramina was headstrong, always had been, even from childhood. Since she was given custody of the house—not ownership, by the way, merely custody— she felt she was entitled to dispose of any contents she didn't see fit to keep there."

"Such as your father's butterflies."

"Yes," Cecile said. "Ramina was ready to sell the whole lot for a pittance and I objected. Of the three of us, only I had knowledge of their true worth and I insisted she find a proper collector. I would have even preferred donating them to a museum, but she wouldn't hear of it. We got into a terrible row."

"And that's when you threatened her?"

Cecile looked at him squarely, not unlike a schoolmarm. "Do you have any family members who vex you, Mr. Shurjack? Sometimes one says things they shouldn't in the heat of the moment." She reached for a tissue from a box on the side table. "I try to be patient, but I'm not a saint, unfortunately." She dabbed at her eyes.

Joe regarded the small presence in front of him.

The tears were real. He had to agree with Joshua, at least on some basic level, that she wasn't capable of murder. Unless he found more to go on, though, she would remain the most likely suspect, especially to the police.

She seemed to be thinking the same. "This isn't going to help my case, is it?"

"I'm not a lawyer, ma'am. You'll need to ask Mr. Baldridge." He gathered his things and put them into his business backpack. "If I can find out what happened to those butterflies—how they left St. Louis and who handled the transactions—I think that trail will help us. Please send me the inventory as soon as you can." He shook her hand, careful not to squeeze the limp fingers offered. "I'll be in touch," he said, handing her a business card.

She looked at it, gave a hint of a smile. "Thank you," she said.

ഇന്ദ

"So," Bea demanded as soon as he hit the door of his Richmond Heights home, "did Lester call you back yet?"

"Lester?" Joe set his backpack down by the kitchen table. "Who's that?"

She gave him an exasperated look. "My mechanic

friend who you said you'd call to check on my car?"

He'd forgotten. "Sorry—I've been busy with the butterfly case."

She pursed her lips. "Look, I don't have forever to get this figured out. You said you'd help."

"I *am* helping—geez, woman, it's like you want me to reorganize the way the world works. Things take time, you know." He suddenly remembered his conversation with Cecile, about family members being difficult sometimes. "Look, I'm sorry. I got busy. I will call this afternoon, I promise."

She didn't look quite placated, but picked up a printout that had been sitting on the counter. "Here's an email from the ALCA."

He opened his mouth to ask what that was.

Bea gave him another of her looks. "The butterfly collector people? They find rare specimens showing up at auctions and other places. This tells about a new exhibit in Albuquerque, New Mexico. Something about a guy who worked for the BioPark who came upon some framed specimens. I guess he loaned them to the Natural History Museum and they're in a new display that's opening soon."

"Albuquerque? I think we drove through there once on our way to California," Joe said, snatching the email. "What the hell is a BioPark?"

Bea crossed her arms. "Well, you're testy today."

"Sorry," he said again. He put the copy down and paced over to the fridge for a beer. The reassuring pop of the can and the fizz that escaped calmed him somewhat. He took a swig. "I've just had a lot of dead-ends lately. This sounds like another one. I mean, people buy and sell things all over the place and I can't check them all out. Those butterflies in Albuquerque aren't necessarily the ones I'm looking for."

"You don't know that for sure. And it'd be nice to get out of town for a while." Bea said. "Best of all, I get to wear some of these new clothes." She gestured toward several shopping bags on the floor.

Joe set his beer down hard, spilling a little. "What? We can't afford—"

"Relax, lover," she said. A curious smile formed on her face. "Teri got the job at the mall, and these were all bought on employee discount. A real steal—not literally, of course."

What in God's name was happening? His whole life seemed out of control. A month ago, he had a steady income and yes, the job was boring and Dressor was an asshole, but it paid the bills. Now he was winging it as a PI—badly, it seemed, and his wife was possessed by his former crazy colleague, and how could it get much worse?

"Joe!" It was Teri's shrill voice. "What is all this?"

She was standing by the bags of clothes. She pulled out a couple—a very short black skirt and a skimpy red top, then removed a sheer nightie. She turned to him, wide-eyed.

Joe shivered. OK, things were now worse—and this was not a direction he wanted them to go, at least not with Bea again. Assuming he'd done it in the first place.

Oh, shit. He didn't have a clue what to do.

Joe smiled, hoping it didn't look fake. "Hey, congrats on the job—and on your new employee discount!"

She drew a deep breath. "I did get the job—and it'll pay so much better than Felding's, especially since they cut my hours so much." Her shoulders slumped. "But I don't remember buying all this or any conversation about it." She trembled. "What is happening to me?"

He instinctively rose and caught her in his arms. "Honey, relax. It'll all be fine." He held her for a while, her lithe form pressed against him. It seemed like eons ago that they'd first met, that he'd held her and kissed her and taken her places. That her incredible smile had won him over, a smile he hadn't seen in a long, long time. And he liked being strong for her when she let him.

She seemed to gather her wits. "I need a glass of wine." She reached and opened a kitchen drawer and pulled out a corkscrew.

"No." He put his hand over hers. "Maybe you shouldn't. Maybe you're just nervous about your job and having to interview and all that." He tapped the back of her hand lightly. "What do you say we get away for a while? I'm probably going to have to go to Albuquerque for a few days. Would you like to go with me?"

Perhaps Bea wouldn't be capable of coming along, in spite of what she said. It might even be good for Teri, give her a change of pace.

She brightened. "Albuquerque? That's only three and a half hours from Raton!"

"Huh?" Joe raised his brows. He was vaguely aware that Albuquerque was somewhere in the state of New Mexico, but didn't know any of the area towns.

Teri beamed. "You know, where the NRA has their big shooting range? The Whittington Center? It's where all the competitions go. I just want to see the place. If you don't have time, I could get a car and drive up there by myself."

"Sure, why not? Tell me, though, when does your new job start?"

"In two weeks, although they enticed me with some benefits that start now."

"Great timing! Let's go, then."

"Yes." She looked at the bags and back to him. "Now, about these clothes—I don't know what I was thinking when I got these! I mean, they're so trashy! Maybe they were on a big sale or something, but it's just not me." She did her one-shoulder shrug. "I'm going to return them."

He smiled weakly. "Whatever you say, honey." He hoped Bea hadn't heard the "trashy" comment.

"Thanks, Joe," Teri beamed. "I mean, for all the encouragement. I think I have been too tense lately. And maybe I'm drinking a little too much vino, you know? But this is so cool—we haven't had a vacation forever!"

"It's not a vacation for me—but you are free to do whatever you want."

Her eyes sparkled. "Raton, here I come!"

It was nice to see her happy for once.

Teri, that is.

Chapter 7

After a very early two-hour flight and checking in at the motel, Joe took off for the BioPark. The museum with the new butterfly acquisitions was closed on Fridays, so this seemed a good way to spend the rest of the morning, looking for the person who provided the specimens.

Teri didn't even leave the airport before renting a car of her own and heading north to the Whittington Center. She seemed cheerful for a change, so Joe just obliged her and took care of all the luggage himself. She said she'd catch up with him later.

So much for any reconnecting!

He paid his out-of-state visitor's fee at the park's entrance and studied a tri-fold map the attendant had handed him. He located the Butterfly Pavilion, stuck the map in his back pocket and started walking toward the center of the park.

For a desert location, there was a lot of green. The botanical garden sat next to the Rio Grande (a mere trickle compared to the mighty Mississippi), but the shade trees surrounding the central grassy area were already sporting summer colors, even in early May. Joe wandered a bit before finding the butterflies, passing through Italianate formal gardens, a model railroad village, even a play castle with a winged dragon and giant ant statues.

It was too bad that Teri took off for Raton as soon as they landed. She probably would have enjoyed the park's whimsy.

As much as she enjoyed anything, Joe reminded himself, except for target shooting. He hoped she was having fun at the Whittington Center—as Teri, not as Bea.

He found the butterfly pavilion and entered the "escape" hallway with doors on both ends. He pushed past the second door and stepped into the huge, netted structure, filled with colorful plants and hundreds of emerging and fluttering butterflies and moths. He unthinkingly swatted at the small black wings that flew near him. The Butterfly Pavilion guard gave him a stern look, but turned to welcome other guests who came in after him.

"And that one's an Erato Longwing, native to northern South America," a male docent with a faded nametag and open guidebook said to a couple of visitors. "It actually eats pollen rather than nectar, so it can live as long as several months." A fit, gray-haired woman in jeans nodded, and then asked about several other butterflies, noting mimicry, habitat and other features.

Joe waited patiently for her to finish. It was curious that people were so into these bugs! Finally, she and her friends, including a grandmother-type in a wheelchair, headed for the exit doors, chattering about the wonderful colors and peaceful setting of the BioPark.

The docent, an older man with silver-gray hair, turned to Joe and pointed out a Great Purple Hairstreak, a fairly large and iridescent bluish beauty. It landed on the concrete path in front of them and folded its wings, showing only its drab brown, spotted underside. "Sort of a two-faced personality," the man said with a grin. "And great for camouflage, too."

Not unlike a lot of criminals, Joe thought. There were always those who were able to cover their looks and fade into the population, making his job harder.

"I'm interested in mounted specimens as well as live ones," he said, pulling out his small notebook and then replacing it. No sense in looking that obvious. "Do you happen to know some collectors around here?"

The docent closed his guidebook and thought for a moment. "I'd have to say check with Walt Merton.

He used to be a curator here, but now works at the Natural History Museum in Old Town. He also leads the local Lepidoptera club. His wife made an incredible find at the flea market, of all places, just about two weeks ago. Found some framed specimens that were pretty old, maybe fifty years or more, probably from someone's estate sale. Walt put a couple on display in the museum and is researching the rest. He was pretty excited about it."

"Yes," Joe answered, trying to play it cool. "I saw on the ALCA website that there was a new exhibit there. Since I was coming to town, I thought I'd try to see it."

"The ALCA? Are you a member?"

Joe shook his head. "Not yet. I'm just getting into it. I've got a lot to learn."

The docent nodded. "Well, Walt's your man. I don't have his phone number with me, but he's in the book—lives in the Nob Hill area. That's near Carlisle and Central, if you're not from around here. You could probably find it on the internet."

Joe thanked him and headed back through the park to his rental car.

Finally, a good lead—maybe. He buzzed the car windows down to let in some cooler air and sat in the driver's seat, making some notes on his phone. Then he began searching both maps of Albuquerque and the online white page listings. What a quaint phrase!—"in the book." Joe smiled. Docents tended to be retired folks, many of whom weren't computer-savvy, so he ought to give the guy a little slack. It wouldn't be long, however, before things like paper telephone books would fade into a forgotten past.

Merton, Walter and Rose. Well, Joe thought, that didn't take long. He called and set up an appointment for later that day. He and Walt would meet in a Central Avenue restaurant for a late lunch—the Dawn Rider Café, across from the University of New Mexico's main bookstore.

Joe started to dial Teri, stopped, hung up, and then decided to dial again anyway.

After several rings, she finally answered. "Hey, Joe! How's it going?"

He hesitated, wondering which woman he was speaking to. "Pretty good. I'm meeting with a butterfly expert in a while, but thought I'd call and see how the shooting range worked out for you."

A distant man's voice came through the speaker: "Second set on top row. Ready—fire!" Snaps and pings flooded his ears.

"Hold on a sec while I step away from the noise," Teri said, and then there was a short pause. "Joe?" she finally said, the background a little quieter, "It's great! I got myself signed up for a competition today! I just did chickens and pigs, and I'm up for turkeys and rams next."

"Sorry?" He didn't understand, but at least it was Teri.

She laughed a little. "Oh yeah, I forget, you're not into this stuff. It's a silhouette shooting competition. It's basically small metal animal cutouts balanced on sticks, and you shoot them in order. Got all of my first two rounds except for one pig, damn it."

The voice in the background called, "Cease fire. Line safe check, please."

Teri continued. "Glad you're having success, Joe, but I gotta go. My line's up next. I'll probably grab a snack after we're done and then head on back to Albuquerque. I should be back by dinnertime, if you want to wait for me. Oh, and they have this cool museum, too, not a huge one, but it's supposed to have a good World Wars pistol exhibit, so I'm going to take a look."

"No problem. I'll meet you back at the hotel. Go get those ducks."

Teri laughed again. "Turkeys. Sorry, no ducks. See ya, Joe."

He pushed the end call button and smiled. She

seemed happy, rare as that was. He hoped it would last a while.

Without Bea, that is.

₨₩

Joe entered the Dawn Rider Café and stopped, surprised. He'd expected an eatery with a Native American or maybe a hot-air balloon decor, both of which were common Albuquerque themes. But this one was a cross between a 1950s hangout and B-Movieland. The restaurant spanned several of what used to be old storefronts, loosely connected with open walkways. The rough wood tables and vinyl booths looked like they'd seen their day quite a while ago, and every wall was decorated with paintings of western cliché cactus, horses, or portraits of John Wayne. Yeah, he'd watched the old shows on TV with his dad, so he knew who John Wayne was. Students, teachers and townsfolk seemed to be the patrons, with many coming and going, studying, talking or eating spicy New Mexican dishes.

Joe wondered if he'd packed some antacids. He'd probably need them later.

A tall, older guy walked in the main door, his hair pulled back into a short gray braid. He looked around and smiled broadly as he saw Joe. "Mr. Shurjack?

Your description of yourself was perfect! Hi, I'm Walt Merton."

The two shook hands, then ordered from the counter. Joe insisted on paying, while Walt took the lead and recommended the chicken enchilada plate with beans and rice. The white-aproned man behind the counter then asked a very strange question: "Red or green?" Walt quickly explained that it was a choice of chile, and said that the green was best. Joe shrugged and trusted his host not to torch too many of his Midwestern taste buds.

They found an empty booth in an adjacent room. Joe slid over a crack in the vinyl seat and noted the people around them: a family with two lively kids, a young couple holding hands, a shaggy-haired man bent over a textbook. Above him, a light board flashed order numbers, letting diners know when their meals were ready. Joe had expected to endure a lot of chit-chat while waiting for their meals, but their number came up rather quickly.

Walt retrieved the food from the serving counter. "Ah, this is a little slice of heaven, my new friend. It's not the fanciest place in town, but you won't find a better meal or price anywhere."

Joe took a bite and felt the burn rise into his nasal cavities. He grabbed for his ice tea, but his host pushed a flour tortilla at him. "Alternate with bites of this—it'll cool you off more than the water, believe me."

After a few more burning bites and wordy niceties, Joe launched into his pitch. "So, I understand you're responsible for a new butterfly exhibit at the Natural History Museum that's starting tomorrow. Rare, mounted specimens, I believe."

"Yes," Walt said, finishing the last of his meal. "We've got spotted lipteals from Uganda, South American two-wings, and double-headed moths."

"Wow," Joe said. "Sounds very exotic. I can't wait to see them."

Walt leaned forward. "Well, you can't."

"Sorry?"

He half-smiled. "None of those are real. I made them up. Besides, butterflies have four wings, not two. Even grade-school kids know that."

The last bite of tortilla caught in Joe's mouth.

Walt's mouth turned downward. "Would you like to tell me who you really are? And what you really want?"

The kids at the table next to them laughed at some joke. The young couple had left. Bea would say he'd blown this one pretty badly. Joe wished he could crawl under the table right then.

"OK," Joe said slowly, deciding on the truth. "I'm looking for a collection of mounted butterflies and moths that was stolen from a home in the St. Louis area about a month ago."

"I thought as much," Walt said, sitting as far back as the narrow booth would allow. "Cop or private dick?"

Joe tried not to cringe at the TV term for his profession. "I'm a professional investigator for an attorney in St. Louis. This theft is tied with a murder, and we're trying to get some evidence to clear a client."

Walt nodded. "I expected something illegal when my wife brought them home from the flea market. I don't know if you're familiar with the collection, but there are several very exotic specimens, things private collectors can rarely afford. You say that they came from a residence in St. Louis?"

"Yes. They were owned by my client's father."

Walt put all his fingertips together. "And somebody got killed because of them?"

"Yes."

He shook his head. "I hate to tell you this, but they didn't belong to your client, whoever he or she was. They were from a museum in Brussels, stolen more than four decades ago. "

"What? How do you know that?"

Walt pursed his lips. "I went straight to the ALCA and researched their online archives. They had some old photos of what was stolen, an exact match for a few of the butterflies and one of the moths. You can tell they're the same by the small rips and tears and repairs—they all leave their mark and can be as individual as a fingerprint."

Joe couldn't believe it. The Burls were bickering over stuff that wasn't even theirs? "They were museum pieces? They must be priceless."

"Not quite priceless. The entire collection would be worth about a couple million dollars today. We, of course, don't have everything, but these were the showpieces." Walt looked at him closely. "You had no idea, did you?"

"Their insurance company put it at $600,000. Apparently that was a little low."

"Apparently," Walt said, rising. "But I intend to return them to their rightful owners. We discourage such collections nowadays, it's so much better to photograph and catalogue rather than capture and kill. But we often run into specimens like this and try to keep them for posterity." He reached into his pocket, producing a card. "Here's my office contact information. I'm sure you'll need some copies of the museum photos to give to your client's insurance company, so feel free to stop by. I should be back there by three o'clock or so."

Joe took the card and looked up. "I don't know what to say. I didn't expect the ownership to be an issue."

Walt shrugged. "Artifact theft can be a nasty business. I'll ask Rosie if she remembers anything about the flea market vendor and let you know. And, by the way, thanks for the meal."

Joe stared at the empty plates after Walt left. This was not going to sit well with Joshua Baldridge, and certainly not with Cecile Burl. Perhaps her father knew all along that the butterflies were stolen. Maybe she did, too, or her sisters did. Or maybe not. And there was possible insurance fraud, and—and—and—

Joe closed his eyes.

The only sure thing was a bad case of heartburn setting in.

ഇ൦ശ

The last of the sun's rays struggled to pierce through the motel room curtains. Joe stacked the photocopied butterfly pictures from his second meeting with Walt, put them into a large envelope, and then tried to organize his thoughts. First of all,

Teri had come back, all excited—she'd won the top prize, in spite of her missed pig—and was now taking a shower. Maybe they could grab a burger somewhere after she got out.

Second, Walt's wife, Rose, had remembered a little about her purchase at the flea market. She was a regular shopper, it turned out, and this had been a new vendor. A lot of the sellers there drove around Albuquerque on the weekends, looking for garage sales and buying underpriced items to later resell at the flea market. So, the butterflies could have come from anywhere.

Joe sighed. Perhaps, if Rose was going to the flea market tomorrow, he could accompany her, find that vendor and ask some questions. He made a quick call to Walt's home and yes, she'd be delighted. Meet at 7:30 a.m., she said, at the main entrance of the State Fairgrounds.

He hung up and stretched, still sitting in the room's only easy chair. He should report in to Joshua, but not until he had all the information. No sense in upsetting everyone at this point.

The door to the bathroom opened, letting out some steam. Teri walked out, her hair still wet. But, unlike at home, where she always swathed herself in a robe, she stood before him absolutely naked.

Joe quickly took in the sight of her slender body—tight breasts, trim hips, that furry patch of light brown hair down low that exactly matched the hair on her head. Teri wasn't one to do anything unnatural, like dye her hair. She was genuine all over.

Nice, he thought, then he noticed she was very focused on him. He swallowed hard.

"Hey, doll," she purred. "Want to know what a champ feels like?"

Before he knew it, she was in his lap, kissing and rubbing. His thoughts grew hazy as she removed his shirt and tugged at his pants.

Wow, they should travel more often, he thought, as she pulled him onto the bed. An almost-forgotten passion overtook them, and he was soon breathing heavily and rhythmically, yielding to the moment.

"Oh!" she sighed, more than once.

They finished and he rolled off of her, amazed at how relaxed he felt. Maybe it'd be good for her to shoot at things regularly. He put a gentle hand on her thigh.

"Was it good for you, sugah?" Teri said with a Bea-like voice.

Joe pulled his hand away like he'd been shocked with megavolts of electricity. "Teri?" he asked.

She just smiled.

Chapter 8

Joe dropped Teri off at a strip mall coffee shop so she could get her morning caffeine fix, then headed toward the fairgrounds. He was glad to be alone, especially after last night. She didn't seem herself, being happier somehow, which he'd initially attributed to her win. But last night, fabulous as it was—

No, he didn't even want to think about it.

The light pinks and blues of the morning sky had just faded as he pulled into the New Mexico Expo's south parking lot. He paid the greasy-haired parking attendant, found a spot near the makeshift tents, and got out to wait for Rose Merton. Walt had shown him a photo of her in his office, so he hoped it wouldn't be too difficult spotting her. He was glad to have something else to think about, so he didn't have to think about—no, he wasn't going to think about—

A short woman came up from one side and tugged at his sleeve. "Shurjack?" she asked.

Once again, he hadn't been paying attention. He turned to the woman with a smile, quickly realizing that the photo in the office had been taken years before. Rose had graying hair and a lot of wrinkles on her face, especially around the edges of her mouth, but she had a friendly way about her that put him at ease.

"Over here." She grabbed his arm and started walking quickly. "I last saw the butterfly seller on the north side of the lot, in a tent with pottery and other stuff."

They wandered past a few stalls, Rose pausing and muttering about having to return to certain bargains before the crowds got there. Suddenly, she stopped short and pointed. "There he is!"

The stall looked like all the others, with folding shelves and display tables and a canvas tent that draped around three sides. There were two very-tattooed people (one was a woman, Joe decided, in spite of the spiky hair, plump build, and similar earrings to the man's), both busy putting out what looked like cheap pottery.

"OK," Rose said, grabbing his arm hard. "You know the good-cop, bad-cop routine? Just keep your mouth shut and follow my lead."

"Wait!" Joe started to say that only experienced interrogators tried such tactics, but she sped ahead of him and confronted the two inked, thirty-something-year-old people.

He hung back a bit, not sure what Rose was up to.

"Hi! Remember me?" she asked, smiling. "I bought a bunch of butterflies all framed up from you."

The man shrugged. "We sell a lot of stuff, lady. If I had that, I don't have no more now."

The woman put down the pot she was dusting and gave Rose a hard look. "Why you asking?"

"Maybe I want more," Rose said coyly.

It didn't convince the sellers. "We don't have nothing like that," the man repeated.

Rose planted herself at the front table. "Or maybe I want to find out where you got them. I heard they were stolen."

The man took a big step out of the tent and loomed over the top of her. It was almost funny, such a large guy next to such a small woman. Joe watched carefully from the next booth over, ready to jump in, if things got rough.

"Look, lady, I run a legit business here. I pay cash for the stuff I sell and I don't ask a lot of questions. These deals are fair and square—I got a license and everything. If you're trying to make trouble for me . . ."

"No," Rose said, not backing down. "I'm not looking for trouble. But maybe I want to return them. I don't want hot stuff, if you know what I mean."

"We don't take no returns." The woman joined the man. "I don't remember you or any butterfly pictures. Get going or I'll call security on you. We don't want no trouble, and believe me, sister, you don't neither."

Rose left, muttering about poor service and stopped a couple of tents away, giving Joe a big wink.

Great, he thought. She's blown any hope of my asking subtle questions and just pissed them off. He sighed and moved to the tent, pretending to look at the pots.

"You and your goddamn brother! Now what's he got us into?" the man said in a low voice.

The woman gave him a fierce look. "You leave him out of this. I was just trying to help. Besides, he's dead."

"Good riddance." The man turned to Joe and spoke in a normal voice. "All those on the front table are $10, these back here are $20. Authentic Indian-made."

Joe sniffed. Sure, if those Indians lived in China. "Sorry, I didn't mean to eavesdrop. Somebody died?"

"Never you mind." The woman quickly wiped away a couple of tears, and went behind the tent. Joe heard rummaging behind the canvas wall, the sounds of cardboard and paper being riffled through. Likely, she returned to her unpacking.

The man shrugged. "Forget her—she's got a 'tude like her brother. The guy drowned a couple days ago."

Joe frowned. "Here? In the Rio Grande?"

The man laughed darkly. "It takes a whole lot of stupid to drown here—or if you're a kid and don't know no better. There's fast water between those sandbars." He grimaced. "Floyd was stupid enough for that, but he drowned back east—in the Mississippi."

Floyd. Back home. Finally, a lead! Joe fumbled at a small blue and green pot. "I'll take this," he said. "Do you have a business card in case I want more?"

The man nodded and handed him a dirty, dog-eared one. "The website is gone, but you can call us on the cell number. We get these pots pretty regular."

"Thanks." Joe pocketed the card and then offered the payment. "And I'm sorry for your loss."

The man shrugged. "One less asshole." He smiled, a few teeth missing, as he took Joe's ten dollar bill. "Have a nice day."

☙❧

Rose rejoined him at a safe distance away from the tent. "Well, did you learn anything?"

Joe nodded. "Yeah, I think I got a lead on who might have been the fence. A relative of those two."

"Good." She looked triumphant. "Now, I'll leave you to your sleuthing. I've got some shopping to do."

"Wait a minute," Joe said. "You were pretty aggressive. You could have blown this whole thing for me."

She smiled. "I didn't, did I? Just call me an astute observer of human nature. I knew what to say to bring them out."

"Then tell me, how is it that you're so brazen and can stand up to people like that? I thought for a minute that he was going to punch you out."

A wicked twitch formed at the edge of her mouth. "I teach first grade at the Catholic school."

"Seriously?"

"Trust me, it's brutal," she said.

&oCR

The dull roar of the airplane engines usually lulled him to sleep, but Joe felt rejuvenated on the way home. He madly scribbled notes about what he planned to look up as soon as he got home. This particular flight didn't have Wi-Fi, and most public venues didn't work for his data services anyway, so his laptop stayed in its case. But he had some real leads. Now that he had the names of the flea market vendors, he could do some searches on them and find out more about the brother, then cross-reference that info with any reports of a drowning in the last week or two.

Teri seemed quiet, more like her depressed self. Joe finished his list and then put a hand on her thigh.

She shuddered.

"What's wrong?" he asked, removing his hand.

"I'm not sure," she said. "I think I'm having blackouts or something. I can't remember stuff."

Uh-oh, he thought.

"I mean, I remember winning the tournament, but I honestly don't remember missing that one pig."

"Maybe you were just excited to be there," Joe offered, hoping it didn't sound lame.

"I don't get it," she said, looking out the fogged plane window. "I'm always really focused when I've got a gun in my hand."

The fellow passenger on the end of their row stiffened. Joe turned to him quickly and said, "Target shooting. She was at a meet."

The man nodded and returned to his novel.

"Honey," Joe said quietly, "maybe we ought to talk about this later."

"That's not everything," Teri said, ignoring him

and pushing on. "I don't remember getting into bed after my shower. And I woke up naked. I never sleep naked. What was up with that?"

The man on the end of the row grunted and looked away.

Joe cleared his throat. "I thought you were tired, so I didn't say anything. Actually," he lowered his voice, "it was kind of nice."

Teri gave him a stern look. "What did you do?"

He pushed back into his seat. "Teri, we're married, for God's sake! It's not unreasonable to sleep together. We did sleep, after all." He decided to omit a few details, like what happened before.

"I don't know what to do." She fidgeted with the latch for the tray-table. "Maybe I ought to see somebody about the blackouts. Maybe it's the drinks. Maybe I ought to quit drinking altogether."

Joe reached over and squeezed her hand. "Whatever you want to do. I'll support you, you know."

"Thanks." She twitched one shoulder. "This sucks, not remembering."

Yeah, Joe thought, it did suck.

But he bet he knew someone who did remember.

Chapter 9

"So," Teri said, her hand on their home answering machine buttons, "who's this guy—a Mr. Hardwell? Looks like he's tried to call you several times."

Joe set down the last suitcase he'd brought in and frowned. "I'm not sure. Write down the number. I'll call him back after I check out a few things I learned in Albuquerque."

Teri scribbled on a pad of paper and handed it to him. "I'll be upstairs, unpacking," she said. "There's a ton of laundry to do from this trip and I might as well get started."

A few minutes later, as soon as Joe busied himself with his computer, Teri returned, sans laundry. Or rather, it was Bea who sashayed into the living room. Those movements were unmistakably hers—as was the irritated expression on her face.

Bea planted herself right in front of him.

"Yes?" he asked cautiously.

"You really need to get to work on my case."

Joe shut his laptop. "Look, I've been busy with the Burls' leads. That case pays the bills." He frowned.

"And it was you who gave me the info about the butterflies possibly being in Albuquerque. I learned quite a bit, thanks to you."

"Yeah, I know." Bea tugged at her tunic. "You found a fence named Floyd. Big deal."

Joe stared. "Crap! So you were there in Albuquerque?"

A hint of blush flashed across her face. "I want to talk about my case."

Joe sat way back in the sofa and rubbed his chin with one hand. "Yeah, I'm sure you do. What about answering my question?"

"What question?"

"What is it with you today? Come on, Bea—spill!"

She sat down in a chair opposite him. "Maybe I don't want to say. Woman's prerogative."

He snorted. "Now that's an outdated term, if I ever heard one!"

"My granny used it all the time—successfully, too, for your information." She leaned forward. "Look, I've got something a little more important to talk about. You may have noticed that Teri's mentioning that she's missing time more often."

"Yeah," Joe said. "She thinks it's because of alcoholic blackouts."

Bea arched Teri's eyebrows. "Well, I'm learning

more about this possession thing. I'm usually aware of what she's doing—"

A sinking feeling hit the pit of his stomach. "About that—did you—"

"Please, just let me get this out." She drew her hands together in her lap. "I think she's becoming more aware of me, too. I'm trying to stay hidden, but it's getting harder. And she's making it more difficult for me to come out."

Holy shit, Joe thought.

"I'm afraid I won't have enough time—" She paused and toyed with Teri's wedding ring. "Lester has called several times."

"Who?"

Bea picked up a paper. "It's on here—Teri wrote the number down for you."

Joe read "Lester Hardwell," a phone number, and a series of ditto marks and looked up. "I don't get it. Who is this guy?"

She gave him an exasperated look. "The mechanic I know? The guy you asked to check my wreck of a car? Apparently he didn't have your cell number because it looks like he left four or five messages on the landline. I think he may have found something. You need to call him right now."

Joe put his hand on the phone, then took it off.

"Look, Bea, I don't like being ordered around. I'm glad to help you, seeing as you're a—spirit now, but don't treat me like Dressor did. You can forget my help in that case."

Bea's eyes sent out sparks. "Don't compare me to that bastard."

"Then be nicer to me."

She threw her hands up. "Look, Joe, I'm sorry, I really am. I'm not used to this whole not-in-my-body thing. All I know is that I have to find out who killed me pretty soon or it'll never happen. I'm frustrated—"

Her tone changed abruptly and the expression on her face fell. "And confused," Teri said. She looked around the living room with glazed eyes. "How did I get down here? Did I just say I'm frustrated?"

Joe let out a slow breath. "Honey, why don't you go lie down? You're probably exhausted from the trip. I'll get us some East Indian take-out after I make a couple of phone calls."

"Okay," Teri said slowly. "I guess that's what I'll do. I don't quite feel like myself." She frowned and turned toward the stairs, stopping at the bottom step. "Um, wake me when you get back with the food."

Joe closed his eyes and swallowed hard. Yeah, no telling which of them he'd be having dinner with.

ഇരൽ

Joshua didn't sound annoyed when told about the trip and the stolen butterflies. For a lawyer given to the dramatic, he was being pretty even. There was a pause on the phone, then he asked, "Anything else?"

"Right now, that's about it," Joe said, tapping a pencil with his free hand. "The apparent fence, Floyd Chapin, drowned here last week, near Eads Bridge. I'm in the process of finding some more background on him."

"Huh? Oh yes, saw the news on the 'net— happened by the riverside Lewis and Clark statue, I believe. Some fool drove his car down the access there."

"That's the one," Joe said. "Pretty weird, though. Don't they usually gate that road off when the river floods?"

"I believe so." Joshua sniffed. "He should have had a clue about the danger, though. According to the photo in the article, the only part of the statue still above water was Clark's hat."

"Takes all kinds, I guess. It'd probably be useful if we could get our hands on the autopsy report."

There was the sound of papers being shuffled. "Let me give you a contact in the M.E. office—Jayne Farr owes me a couple of favors. Mention my name when you call her."

"Great!" Joe scribbled down the information. "And thanks."

"By the way," Joshua continued, "Cecile Burl called yesterday. She got a call from a collection agency, looking for Meris. Seems our party girl has a gambling habit besides being a free spender, and she owes somewhere in the low six figures."

Joe whistled. "With her income and assets? Wow."

"Not everyone is a good money manager, that's for sure. If that were the case, I'd be out of business."

Unbelievable, these Burl sisters, Joe thought. He suddenly felt like he lived on an entirely different planet than these unhappy rich women.

"Speaking of assets," Joe said, "do you think the sisters knew the butterflies weren't really theirs?"

Joshua laughed. "It'll certainly make an interesting conversation. Are you free tomorrow afternoon, say, about four o'clock? You and I could drop in and have a chat with Cecile and Meris, if they'd agree to be in the same room together. It'd be right in time for tea."

Joe thought about Meris' lack of manners the last time he'd been at the mansion. Maybe Joshua's presence would improve their visit, although he wasn't going to count on having any teatime goodies.

"Sounds good. I should know more about Floyd Chapin by then, too."

He touched the "end call" button on his cell and set it down among the strewn papers on his coffee table. People and their stuff—and other people wanting the same stuff—it was the same old story, whether it was a murder in St. Louis or a full-scale war overseas.

The landline rang and Joe grabbed it, hoping it didn't wake Teri. He checked his watch. It was almost seven o'clock and he hadn't gotten the take-out yet. Hopefully this wouldn't last long.

"Hello?" he asked.

"Joe Shurjack? This is Lester Hardwell. I been tryin' to get hold of you."

Joe sat down quickly and cradled the phone with his shoulder. He grabbed a notepad and pen. "Yeah, sorry about that. I was out of town. What did you find?"

"You got a problem here—those brake lines were definitely cut."

"Really? Oh, shit!"

He glanced heavenward and closed his eyes for a moment. Bea was right—someone had deliberately caused her death. It made him angry and sad, a strange mix, even though the possibility had been in front of them for some time.

He let out a long sigh. "Hey, I really appreciate your checking this out. Can I ask you to do one more favor? I need to have some proof, like a photo."

"I did better than that," Lester replied. "I took 'em with me."

Joe about dropped the phone. "Oh god—you didn't—"

"Sure did. Cut 'em out myself." There was a note of pride in Lester's voice. "Want me to bring 'em over?"

Of all the stupid—so much for the investigation! The brakes were now worthless as evidence. Joe recovered, thanked the hapless mechanic, gave him his address, and hung up.

He held his head in his hands and sat, taking several deep breaths. *OK, so that didn't work out like you'd hoped. Think, man. There must be another way to attack this.*

He straightened and grabbed paper and pen. First off, Bea was murdered; it was clear now that it was no accident. Her car was indeed tampered with, even though they couldn't prove it.

But the fact that she was murdered, well, that changed everything.

He scribbled her name and drew several lines

under it.

And what else had he learned? Smitters falsified the original police report on the condition of the car. He wrote that down. Why had he done that? Ineptitude? Simple greed? Or something more sinister?

Joe tapped the pen. Bea had said that Smitters was on the payroll with Dressor, too. Perhaps he could ask Chuck to get him some of those records. Chuck was a quasi-relative and the sole employee left after Dressor's firings, but Joe knew he wasn't enamored with either the job or the boss. But, would Chuck help? Or would he tip the old man off?

He drew a big question mark next to Chuck's name. He also needed some info about Bea's last cases.

Bea hadn't remembered much about what she was working on at the time of her death. Just routine stuff, she'd said. And nothing was going on in her private life that anyone would have had it in for her. Yet, what had she inadvertently seen, or overheard, and who would have something to lose for it? Somehow, she'd been a threat to someone.

More question marks. Joe shook his head. He was missing something. This wasn't coming together at all.

And what of that mystery woman, the one Hector

Gonzales told him about? Was she just a paying customer at the garage or was she involved somehow? And who the hell was she?

He drew a hand with a strawberry on it, then threw the pen down. "How about a break?" he said aloud to the ceiling fan above him. "I could use some help here."

It just whirred.

Chapter 10

Joe turned off his car's wipers and parked in front of the Burl mansion. He hadn't been able to sleep much with so many spinning thoughts, and he felt as foggy as the weather. At least this case was moving along, although he wasn't excited to be back at the scene of the crime. He glanced out the windshield. The limestone exterior of the old home took on a gray cast in the drizzle. Even the windows seemed dark and uninviting.

Much like its occupants.

Joshua had beat him there by a few minutes and was already seated in an overstuffed armchair in the drawing room, the same pretentious room where Joe had first met Meris. The maid entered with a tray full of teacups and pastries, then announced the sisters. The two entered, separately, and took up battle-stations across the room from each other.

"I've got some important news about the collection," Joshua said, standing. "Perhaps we could convene in the center of the room, closer to the tea service?"

"Of course," Cecile said quietly, rising from her corner. "Where are my manners? Please, help yourself, gentlemen."

Joshua poured tea with a flourish and handed cups to the sisters, and then to Joe. Meris slunk across the room like a cat guilty of leaving a hairball somewhere, and took her cup without a word. Cecile nodded her thanks and sat down facing her sister, her legs angled together in a lady-like pose.

Joe had to admire Joshua's style and his ability to get the two warring parties closer together, although the tension in the room was as thick as the sky outside.

"I hope this won't take long. I've got an appointment to get my nails done with a rather exclusive salon. I've had to wait days to get in," Meris grumbled. She was dressed in casual slacks and a sloppy tunic, but looked slightly better than when Joe had seen her last. "What's the poop?"

Joshua cleared his throat, lawyer-like. "Mr. Shurjack, here, has done extensive research and turned up some rather startling facts about your father's collection." He turned to Joe.

Oh great, Joe thought. *Make me the bad-news guy.* He also cleared his throat. "I was able to find a few of the stolen butterflies in New Mexico, of all places.

They'd been sold by a fence from St. Louis and turned up in a flea market."

"Good heavens!" Cecile put her hand on her chest.

Meris peered over her teacup. "Oh, give me a break, Cecile! Did you think they'd turn up at Sotheby's or Christie's? If you ask me, you're way too possessive of Daddy's things."

Cecile gave her an icy stare. "Did I ask you anything? I was not aware that I was even talking to you!"

"Bitch!" Meris muttered, not quite under her breath.

"Ladies, ladies," Joshua broke in, a practiced smile on his face, "I believe Mr. Shurjack has more to tell you."

Joe choked on a bite of very dry pastry. "I—just a moment." He swigged down the rest of his tea before he gagged. "Excuse me. The fence's name was Floyd Chapin, and apparently he was the man who drowned by the Louis and Clark statue last week."

Cecile frowned. "I think I heard something about that—"

"Not me, I never read the papers." Meris stuffed a piece of croissant in her mouth. "So what?" she said, her words muffled.

Curious, Joe thought. Neither woman seemed to recognize Floyd's name. "According to the police report, he was suspected of committing several burglaries in U-City and the Central West End. The footprints found in a side room here match his shoe size, and there were some fingerprints on the back door. The police are trying to determine if he was the person who shot your sister."

Cecile's face lit up. "Then, I am free and clear?"

Joshua grimaced slightly. "Not quite, I'm afraid. He was a hired thug, so we still have to prove you didn't contract with him to do the deed."

"That's ridiculous!" Cecile snorted, very unladylike. "Why on earth would I do that?"

Meris raised her eyebrows. "Why on earth, indeed, my dear sister!" she said, mocking her. "Maybe because you hated her having control of the house?"

Cecile gave her a condescending look. "Oh, and you two were best friends? I'm surprised that both of you didn't sell off most of the paintings and artwork. By the way, where is that large Ming vase"—she said it like 'vahs'—"that used to stand in the entry hall?"

Meris sneered. "Maybe it went back to the same consignment store she bought it at. Half the stuff in here is fake, you know."

"Speaking of fake," Joshua interrupted, "you'll find this quite interesting. We also learned that your father's butterfly collection was originally from a museum in Belgium. An expert in Albuquerque confirmed it and discovered that the specimens were stolen from there nearly half a century ago."

"What!!" both sisters said at once.

"Those came from Uncle Curt!" Cecile said, too loudly.

"Oh, shit!" Meris turned toward her sister. "Uncle Curt worked somewhere in Europe, didn't he?"

Cecile went pale. "Antwerp or Brussels, I forget which. This just can't be!" She turned toward Joshua. "And the insurance money we collected for the butterflies?"

He nodded grimly. "It will have to be returned."

"What the fuck!" Meris exploded. "I can't believe this!"

"Why? Were you hoping to pay off your Las Vegas debts?" Cecile said sharply.

It was Meris' turn to turn colors—in her case, an uneven red. "How do you know about that? Have you been poking around in my business?"

Joshua motioned to Joe. "What do you say we let that last bit sink in?" he said, quietly.

The two ducked into the nearby hall as the sisters

grew louder.

Joe turned his head away from the shouting. "How would you like to proceed from here? I don't think either sister was involved with that fence. Neither one reacted when I said his name."

"I agree. When Meris calms down a bit, ask what consignment shop Ramina dealt with. I have a feeling that the belongings here were treated—shall we say, rather fluidly? I'm not sure that information will get us much, but it may give us an idea of the type of people she worked with."

Joe did a quick side-step as Cecile stormed out of the room. She swept through the hall toward the front door, and soon he heard a slam. He turned to Joshua. "This family is a financial disaster and it's going to take a while to untangle everything. Perhaps Cecile might help us access Ramina's records as well. When she's calmed down," he added.

"Yes, that might take a while," Joshua said, nodding. "Call me tomorrow if you learn anything. I'll also send you another check to cover your Albuquerque trip." He grinned. "Who knew butterflies could be so entertaining?"

Entertaining. Joe shook his head. That wasn't his word for it.

&)(&

As soon as he got home, Joe's cell rang. It was Chuck Amstead, from Dressor's office. "Hey, man, I was about to call you," Joe said.

"This is going to sound a bit strange, and I need your discretion," Chuck said, almost whispering. "Uncle Don is out of the office, but I expect him back any minute." He paused. "I need your help—I think he's cheating on Annie."

Joe toyed with a pencil. "Did she call you?"

"No, my mom called and said Aunt Sofie was worried that he's cheating on Annie. Annie's her sister-in-law, you know."

OK, it was that convoluted relationship thing again, Joe remembered. "So, what would you like me to do? Tail him, take some pictures?"

Chuck's voice was even softer. "I told Mom I'd check it out, but there's no way I can do it myself. I'll pay you."

Joe glanced at his sketches and notes about Bea's case, and the question marks near Chuck's name. "Actually, I've got a better idea. I need some info that might be on past payrolls. We could trade services."

There was a long pause. "OK, Joe, as long as nothing's illegal. But let's do it this way: you get me photos, and then I'll give you whatever you want."

"Done." Joe listened and wrote down what Chuck

knew about Dressor's paramour, but was abruptly cut off. Dressor must have returned to the office.

He stared at his notes. "White woman, short red hair, about 45 years old, medium-heavy build, stylish clothes." And Dressor had already announced that he was "working" late tonight, even though Chuck knew he had no cases that weren't already headed to court.

Joe grabbed his car keys and camera. Looked like he'd be working late himself.

Chapter 11

Joe turned on his phone's voice recorder. "Subject left the Coleridge Building at 7:10 p.m., then drove to the northwest parking garage near the Convention Center. At 7:30 p.m., he came out of the garage and walked a few blocks to the Pie Town Pizza restaurant on Washington, entering same." Joe watched as several other patrons also entered and left: an African-American family with two squirmy kids; two almost identical gray-haired women (probably sisters or cousins, Joe guessed); a young blond man wearing a business suit, accompanied by two other similarly-suited companions; three high-school or young college women, all clad in jeans and matching tees, and many more ordinary St. Louis folks. More than an hour later, just when his own stomach began to rumble—why didn't he think to bring a sandwich?—Dressor left with a red-haired woman on his arm.

Bingo! Joe quickly snapped a couple of photos from the side window of his Honda. He set the camera down and slowly drove into a no-parking zone, grateful that the cops weren't working the area just now. Soon Dressor's dark-blue Lexus appeared at the parking garage's exit and took off to the south. Joe followed them to Forest Parkway and settled back to a comfortable distance between their car and his.

Once they were past Washington University's undergraduate campus, with its Oxford-like stone buildings, the road became controlled-access, so he was less likely to lose them. Joe had to drive a little faster than he liked in this usually-patrolled area, but again, fortunately, no cops were there at this hour.

At the end of the parkway, the Lexus took the off-ramp to north 170, then veered into the left lane. Joe frowned. Were they headed to the airport?

The signs for Lambert International Airport came overhead, and still the Lexus plowed on. Joe shrugged and switched to a middle lane, holding back as far as he could.

Following a dark car on a dark, overcast night was no picnic. Joe finally slid into the left-hand exit lane, two cars behind his quarry.

Suddenly, the Lexus lurched out of the lane and crossed several white lines to return to north 170, barely dodging a double-semi in the process. It was too late for Joe to do the same. He rounded the exit ramp to find himself stuck in a slow-down right by the airport. *Damn!*

Well, that was it for this evening. Several minutes later, Joe got off at Lindbergh and found a place to pull over. He flipped on the camera and thumbed the control to see what he'd captured. Dressor's image was clear enough to see that it was him; the woman had her back to the camera, so all that showed was the back of her hair and a rather bold floral skirt.

Not much to go on.

From the way he'd driven, Dressor may have seen him. Or else he was one of the many bad drivers in the St. Louis area. Joe couldn't take that chance, however. He also knew this kind of surveillance would take several evenings of his time. Tomorrow, he'd borrow Teri's VW and try again.

ഇന്ദ്ര

After a few nights, he had some pictures, but not the incriminating ones Chuck needed: Dressor and the woman eating frozen custard at Ted Drewes, dining at an Italian restaurant on the Hill, munching tapas at an outdoor café downtown.

Didn't these people do more than eat? Joe wondered. There were no movie dates or motel rendezvous. No impassioned embraces, no kissing. What kind of affair was this?

As he followed them to the Boat House in Forest

Park the next afternoon, Joe thought about calling Chuck and ending the deal. Maybe Chuck would find him the records he needed anyway, just for being a good sport. Dressor was as boring in love as he was in person.

The dark blue Lexus parked in a handicapped spot and the two got out. Joe hated people who did that, making it difficult for people who really needed those spaces.

The woman was wearing yet another bold print dress, this one striped like a zebra. Too bad they didn't go to the Forest Park zoo, Joe thought, as he spotted a legal parking place. She'd blend right in.

He parked and then walked to a vantage point far to the west of the paddleboat dock. The two were in the restaurant section—where else?—under the umbrellas that overlooked the lagoon, the ducks, and the intrepid few who rented the unwieldy leg-powered boats.

However, someone else was with them this time. Joe leveled his camera and took a few pictures, then zoomed in to see who it was.

Pete Smitters! What the hell?

Through his electronic eye, Joe could see an envelope being passed to Smitters, then the three of them left, one at a time—Dressor in his car, Smitters in his, and the woman on foot.

Joe decided to follow the woman this time. She boarded the gaudy tourist bus that ran through Forest Park and stopped at various spots of interest. Joe sprinted to his car and began following the bus. It stopped at the Jewel Box conservatory, the Planetarium, the World's Fair Pavilion—no sign of her getting off. Finally, past all the museums, golf course, visitor center and fields, she disembarked at the Metrolink Station at DeBaliviere Street. Joe pulled into a commuter parking lot, slammed the door shut and bolted for the station. But before he could get to the platform, she was gone on the next train west.

Joe panted at the Metrolink's entrance. He'd lost her again.

ഇൽൽ

Joe sifted through notes, texts and phone messages. There'd been no news on Bea's case, but Cecile had come through with Ramina's bank records, including a copy of her checkbook. From that he learned that the consignment shop that Ramina had been using to sell off the family heirlooms was Lotus Moon Antiques, way out in St. Charles, Missouri.

At least he was getting paid for his mileage.

The results of his skip-tracing on Meris confirmed

that she did owe a large sum of money ($250,000, not including interest), she'd been arrested for marijuana possession twice, and she hadn't had a real job in more than a decade. Cecile was due for a big balloon payment on her drab but elegant home and was behind in taxes as well. Both sisters had motives for getting the insurance money on the butterfly collection; but neither one was strong enough to warrant murder, given their large "allowances."

"Bah!" Joe threw down the many notes and shut his computer lid with a bang. Between this case and Bea's unsolved murder, he was getting nowhere.

"Why don't you come to bed?" Teri asked. She stood at the foot of the stairs, clad in a thin bathrobe. "You've been puzzling over that stuff for days."

Joe glanced at her—it did seem like Teri, and he was very tired. "Sure, honey. Be up in a minute."

She nodded with that sad little smile she always wore, and padded upstairs.

Maybe Dressor was right, maybe he didn't have what it took to be a PI, certificate or no. Joe turned out the lights and headed to bed.

Or maybe what he needed was a break. The right clue could solve a case, he knew. He just had to be smart enough to find it.

The bedroom seemed strangely lit, then he

noticed that Teri had put candles on the windowsills. "What's this?" he asked.

She shrugged one shoulder. "They sell them at my store. The scent is supposed to give serenity and relax you."

He smiled. That was thoughtful. He had been working pretty hard. And tonight, well, he just felt spent. It would be heaven to get a good night's sleep.

He brushed his teeth, got his pajama bottoms on, and slid into bed next to Teri. She seemed immobile, almost not breathing. Well, Joe thought, so much for a good night kiss. That would have been nice. But maybe she was tired, too. He closed his eyes.

Suddenly she turned to him, her nightclothes gone. Before he knew what was going on, her lips were on his, soft and probing, her mouth open, her tongue touching his—

"Oh!" he moaned as she put her hand into his pajamas.

Joe forced himself to look into her face, really look, and it didn't seem like Teri. There was a confidence she didn't have, a determination to have her way with him that Teri never expressed.

"Damn you, Bea," he whispered, not moving away.

"Shut up," she replied.

Chapter 12

If the Central West End could be considered kitsch, then St. Charles, Missouri, could be said to have an enforced quaintness to it. Joe drove over the cobbled streets, dodging gawking tourists huddled under umbrellas. Main Street was a shopper's haven, with uncountable curiosity stores and specialty restaurants, many in aged brick buildings with shutters. Some were actual historic buildings and some were made to look that way. It made for a pretty town on a nice day. But it was raining again (lovely Midwestern weather!), so today it looked old and gray.

He turned off Main onto Pike street and soon came to Lotus Moon Antiques. A narrow drive led to a large lot behind the store, so he parked and walked around to the front.

The display windows were filled with all things celestial: grinning moon lamps from the 1950s, posters with starlets dangling from crescent moon cutouts, astronaut dolls, furniture with stars and moons carved into their backs. There were moon storybooks, novels, comic books; T-shirts, boxes, clocks; mobiles and lots of artwork. Joe shook his head. Obsession, anyone?

He opened the door, ringing a small moon-shaped bell. A pleasant-looking thirtyish woman wearing a large white apron came up to greet him. "Welcome to Lotus Moon! Please feel free to browse and let me know if you need anything," she said, smiling. He nodded and proceeded to poke around.

Unlike the front of the store, the back half was filled with non-moon-themed merchandise of all kinds—junk, his mom would have called it. Probably like many other shops, the term "antique" was rather loosely used, Joe thought. Anything that looked somewhat worn or old seemed to be game here.

The saleswoman greeted another customer, so Joe took the opportunity to go farther back into the store, into a short hallway that led outside to the parking lot. There, leaning against the wall, were two craft paper-covered artworks. He fingered the loose coverings and stole a look at them—one was a lake with a boat in the distance, one an old-fashioned scene with country house, trees and cows—both in intricate frames.

"Excuse me?" came a harsh voice. "This area is for staff only."

He stiffened and looked up. The clerk he'd met earlier flashed a look between consternation and panic.

"Oh, sorry," he said. "I was looking for a nice landscape and saw this one. How much is it?"

"It's not for sale," she said, then softened her tone. "What I mean is, it's already sold. I do have some others up front, though, which I can show you. You're interested in watercolors, then?"

"Yes, of course," Joe replied, happy to play along. He hadn't gotten a really good look to know what they were.

The woman ushered him out of the hallway and up to an area near the cash register. She thumbed through some shrink-wrapped prints in a large bin. "I've got a few Turners, and there's a Constable and Monet as well. I'm afraid the last two are oil reproductions, though."

"No originals?" Joe asked. "The ones in the back looked like originals."

"Those are few and far between," she answered. "We almost never have anything but prints. I was told that those paintings in the back are a very good quality print called giclée. Looks very authentic, especially if you put them in an expensive frame." She gestured toward the bin. "Do you see anything you like here?"

Joe gave each of the proffered artworks a

lingering glance. "No, these aren't quite what I had in mind. But thanks, anyway."

The woman gave a perfunctory smile. "Let me know if you need help with anything else."

"I will. By the way, I enjoyed your front display with all the moon things. Very creative."

This time she gave a genuine smile. "It's a nod to the owner's mother, who started the shop. In fact, it's named after her. She was fascinated by the space race back in the 1960s—it really captured her imagination."

"Lotus Moon was her name?"

"Yeah, she was kind of a hippie, I guess. Her daughter—the present owner—is just the opposite. She's all business." She looked away as an older woman came in. "Be right with you," she called out.

"Listen, don't let me take up all your time. Thank you for the tour and the art lesson." Joe gave his sincere smile. "Do you mind if I grab a business card?"

She smiled and handed him one. "Come back. You never know what you'll find here."

Joe headed out the front door and made his way toward the parking lot. It seemed that it was just an ordinary consignment/resale shop. There was nothing unusual, except that the rain had finally stopped.

While he sat in his car making notes, a dark-haired woman in a leopard print skirt—*what was it about these animal prints this year?*—came out the back door. He slouched way down in his seat, hoping she didn't see him. She was carrying the two artworks that he'd been shooed away from. She clicked open the trunk of a BMW sedan and lay them in quickly, then shut it, looking around. She then ducked back into the store, but not before he snapped a couple of photos of her.

Perhaps she was merely getting ready to deliver them to her client, Joe thought. He jotted down her license plate, the time, and other details anyway.

೨೦೧೪

On the phone, Chuck promised to email details of Bea's last cases, even though Joe hadn't quite nailed Dressor. "I'll keep working on it," Joe said.

"Thanks," Chuck said. "He's slippery, not surprised you're having problems finding much. And you're right—lunches or dinners with another woman don't mean more than a business deal. By the way, the stuff I'm sending you has some info on partial recoveries. I think Bea's last two cases involved thefts and insurance claims, rather routine I'm afraid."

Joe frowned. "Hey, Chuck—tell me, do you remember if we've ever found everything on a recovery case? Seems like they're always partials."

"That is weird when you think of it. I mean, some things get fenced right away and are 'lost,' but we should be able to retrieve a whole set once in a while. I can't remember ever doing that."

"Oh well, thanks for everything. I'll be in touch as soon as I learn more."

Joe hung up. So many loose ends, on both Bea's and the butterfly cases!

He made copies of his St. Charles photos and spread them all over the coffee table, along with his various notes. There had to be some way to make sense of all this.

Teri walked in, sipping an ice tea. "Still puzzling over your cases?"

"Yeah," he said, running his fingers through his hair. "Just doesn't come together. I know I'm missing something here."

"Mind if I take a closer look?" she asked.

Joe regarded her. She rarely showed interest in what he was doing and her question actually pleased him quite a bit. "Sure, but you can't say anything to anybody. It is an investigation, after all."

She nodded and leaned in closer. "Is that Dressor?" she asked.

"Not giving you any specifics. Sorry!"

"OK, I'll be good," she said. She started studying a photo of the Lotus Moon owner. "Oh, my god!"

"What?" Joe said quickly.

She set down her glass. "That's an IZB!"

"A what?"

Teri pointed to the woman's skirt. "Ignatz Bento—you know, the famous designer?"

He must have had a clueless look on his face because she pursed her lips and shook her head. "You have no idea what I'm talking about," she said.

"Yeah, clothes have always been your kind of thing."

Teri tapped the photo. "Ignatz Bento—really expensive and really exclusive. He's got a shop in London, Paris, and New York. You have to have an appointment just to see the clothes. They cost thousands. It's like buying a Rolex—it's only for a very elite clientele. Can't buy it over the 'net or any other way."

Joe frowned. "How do you know it's not some knock-off?"

Teri gave him a condescending look. "I do have an associate's degree in fashion, remember? It has to do with the hemline and the fit and the pattern of the print. It's never been copied quite right. Besides the purse she's carrying clearly has his initials on it—see?

IZB."

Joe leaned over for a closer look, and sure enough, Teri had it pegged. "Why," he wondered aloud, "would a resale shop owner in St. Charles be wearing such expensive clothes? Come to think of it, she also drove one of the newer model BMWs."

Teri shrugged. "Business must be good."

"Not that good. You should have seen what she was selling at her store. Reprints, comic books, old furniture and stuff."

She sniffed. "Yeah, and that's a lousy wig she's got on, too."

"Wig?!"

"Yeah." She pointed to two different photographs taken in the Lotus Moon parking lot. "Look at the part. Here it's on the left, and here it's toward the middle. Her hair's uneven, longer on this side in this photo, but not in this one."

Joe stared at the photos. She was right.

"And this red-haired woman, here, the one with Dressor? She's got an IZB skirt on, too. What are the chances of that? Two women in St. Louis County with clothes like that, with the same build? And if I'm not mistaken, these skirts are special summer releases. Hardly anyone has them yet."

Joe grabbed her and gave her a big, sloppy kiss.

Teri wiped her mouth but gave him a sly look. "What was that for?"

He beamed. "I think you just cracked my case!"

Chapter 13

Joe stopped working for a moment and arched his back to get a good stretch. It was dark and the house was quiet, and he wondered what time it was. Joe glanced at his computer clock: *11:30 p.m.*

He reached for his half-finished beer and drank a little. He needed to stay clear-headed, so he wouldn't get another one. Joe put the can on the coffee table, next to his laptop and a growing pile of evidence. This was the unglamorous part of being an investigator — looking up info and puzzling out everything. He was so close to a solution, if he could only tie a few things together.

He opened his email and found a forwarded memo from the U-City police department, via Joshua's office. The ballistics report indicated that the bullet that killed Ramina came from the same kind of pistol that Floyd Chapin owned. Their conclusion was that he most likely was the killer — given that his fingerprints were on the door jamb and his shoe size fit the footprints in the hall. Joe half-smiled. The footprints had been his tip. So, in the end, they said, it was a burglary gone bad.

Joe scratched his head. It was a pretty amateur job, overall. Only kids or crack heads would be so careless as to leave that much evidence or use a registered gun, dead body or no.

It also didn't answer the question about why only the butterfly collection was taken, and nothing else of value was—not even Ramina's expensive watch, which was in plain sight.

He fumbled through the stack of papers. Floyd Chapin's autopsy report had come in from the coroner friend of Joshua's. Floyd's neck had broken in the accident, it said. The watery Mississippi made it harder to determine the exact time of death, but a surveillance camera a block away had recorded his vehicle speeding by at about 1:30 at night. After the bars close. The body had a significant level of alcohol in it, and no water in the lungs.

Joe raised his eyebrows. No water in the lungs? That meant he broke his neck first—or it was broken for him. The various bruises on the body suggested some kind of trauma. Nothing really leapt out as inconsistent with such an accident, though. Still, it was curious that he died so soon after the botched burglary.

He picked up Ramina's bank statements from

among the papers that Cecile had sent him. There were a few checks for significant amounts, but the statement didn't indicate more than that. Thankfully, Cecile had also provided some of the actual registers, so he now cross-referenced those.

He studied the neat handwriting and noted the names. Apparently the mansion needed a lot of repairs—there were numerous payments to various contractors. That wasn't unusual for those century-old places, and updating them was anything but cheap. Some of the amounts were many tens of thousands of dollars.

So she was fixing the place up—to sell it, maybe? Well, Ramina had been named the executor of the Burl estate. All of that was legal, as long as she shared the proceeds with her sisters.

He shuffled through the other papers from Cecile and found a thick document with appraisals of household art and other items. Cecile had told him that Ramina had the most business sense of the three of them, so perhaps that was why she felt it was necessary to get a value on everything. Cecile had also said that her sister was bent on selling off a lot of the home's contents, which none of them really wanted. He flipped through the long lists.

Stuck unobtrusively in the middle of the list, a

value of $600,000 for the butterflies, which of course was way less than they were actually worth.

He sniffed. So Ramina damn well knew that the butterflies were worth something. She may have been cleaning house, so to speak, but she knew what she was dealing with.

Did she know they were stolen from the museum? Joe wondered. If so, she also would have known she couldn't sell to collectors. And a place like the Lotus Moon wouldn't have given her close to its appraised value. At least not in the front sales room.

Unless there was something else going on. Something that involved expensive paintings in the back hall.

On a hunch, Joe did another search on Floyd Chapin, using his newer data services. Floyd came up as a "person of interest" in several area burglaries, but nothing had been filed against him. Joe sat back and thought for a moment. Something about those paintings at the Lotus Moon didn't sit right with him. He did another search combining burglaries and paintings and came up with a newspaper article in the St. Louis Post-Dispatch from a month ago.

"Elderly Couple Robbed of Priceless Paintings," the headline said. Apparently they'd gone on vacation and returned to find the home ransacked. The paintings stolen were 19th century English watercolors by several artists. A photo of the couple in happier days in their living room showed a few of the now-gone items.

Joe frowned. He clicked the magnifying icon and zeroed in on one of the paintings behind the couple. He couldn't be one-hundred percent sure, since all he'd gotten was a glimpse, but it looked like the same lake picture that he'd seen in the Lotus Moon's back hall, fancy frame and all.

"Giclée, my ass," he muttered.

He picked up the check registers and scanned them for the Lotus Moon. There were several deposits from the shop, presumably for items she sold them. The amounts varied but were substantially higher than what he would have guessed by the average prices around the front showroom. Was a backroom operation was taking place, or was it merely a special selection for an elite clientele?

And was Dressor involved somehow? If the shop owner was the same woman who had dined all around town with him, then what was his part in all this?

Joe felt a headache coming on. Yeah, it was getting too late to think clearly about anything at this point and he might as well go to bed. He could do some more research in the morning.

Footsteps sounded on the stairs and a sleepy Teri/Bea frowned at him. "What are you doing up so late?"

He shrugged. "Just trying to figure things out."

A coy look came over her face. "On my case or the Burls'?"

Bea. He really didn't want to deal with her right now. He didn't like that he'd slept with her, even though it'd felt good at the time. Even though it was Teri's body. Somehow, that made it worse. He didn't like making mistakes and certainly didn't like repeating them, which seemed like all he was doing at the moment.

"Well, sugah?" Bea loosened the tie on Teri's satin bathrobe, revealing some lacy bits beneath.

He drew a long breath and deliberately looked back at his computer. "I was working on the Burl case tonight. I'm meeting Chuck tomorrow—he said he had some information that might relate to your last cases."

Bea sat down opposite him, her robe fully open now, exposing a fancy pink bra and panties. "Great! When and where do we meet him?"

Joe raised his eyebrows. "Huh? No way are you coming with me. It would be very unnatural for Teri to be there."

Bea stood up, pouted, and then sashayed around the coffee table. She sat down close to him and leaned forward. "Unnatural? Maybe you'd like a little more natural right here on the sofa?" She reached a hand for his lap.

"No!" He jumped up and took a few steps back. "I'm sorry, but I can't do this. It's not fair to Teri."

She looked at him like he was crazy, then rewrapped her robe. "Well, you're in a mood, aren't you? I'm not used to men turning me down."

"I'm sure that's true," he muttered. "Look, we're friends. We ought to act like friends. Period."

"Fine," she said abruptly. "Then you better sleep down here tonight."

"Whatever." He sat down on the easy chair.

Bea's face sagged to Teri's for just a second, then returned to Bea again.

Joe shot to his feet. "What the hell?"

Bea frowned, then looked straight at him. "She's aware of me. Not specifically, but she's aware that someone else is taking over for a while. And she's pushing on me, trying to come out even now. That damn shrink she just started seeing set her going, I'm sure."

"And what can we do about it?"

"Pretty much nothing."

Joe sat down again and bent over, running fingers through his hair. This was all he needed, now—another huge distraction and a real worry about Teri finding out.

Bea sighed. "Well, just thought I'd warn you about Teri. Looks like it'll be another lonely night—for all of us." She headed back upstairs.

Joe waited until she was gone, then grabbed an afghan and turned out the light. He probably should have told her he had a headache, which was true, instead of telling her how he really felt. But he was done with this pseudo-affair. And he was going to work a little harder on Bea's case so he could be done with her, too. She had strained their friendship way too far.

He pulled the afghan up to his chin. His feet stuck out the other end.

Damn, he thought, as he tried to fall asleep.

Chapter 14

Joe awoke to the sound of a slamming door. He blinked several times, a little disoriented, and then remembered that he'd been relegated to the couch last night.

By Bea.

Note to self, he thought, as the lumpy cushions nagged at his back—*we need to buy a new couch.*

He stretched out an arm, hitting the coffee table. Ouch. And did he need an explanation for Teri as to why he didn't come to bed? He thought for a moment. Nah, she'd probably just assume that he'd been working too hard and fell asleep down here. It'd happened before, so it wasn't much of a stretch to tell her that. If she asked, that is.

Joe unfolded himself and sat up, yawning. He glanced at the hall clock and saw it was only 7:30 in the morning. He frowned. The door he'd heard was the one to the garage. Where was she going so early? Teri rarely got up before 8:00. One benefit of working at boutique stores was that they tended to open a little later than the big boxes.

He grabbed his phone and found a text from her: *Running errands, see you after work.*

Well, that answered that.

Another message beeped through, from Chuck: *Meeting today needs to be at 9:10 a.m. sharp. City Museum, insect room. Need directions?*

He answered "Yes" and then set his phone down. Why the weird time? Chuck was certainly getting dramatic about a little info exchange. And why the City Museum, of all places?

Joe changed into fresh clothes, grabbed some coffee and headed downtown through the drizzle of another crappy weather day. The City Museum was only a few blocks from where he used to work. It was, however, a place frequented by almost everyone with kids. Rather than the usual historical relics, this "museum" was part eclectic collections and part playhouse and amusement park.

Oh well, Joe thought. Most museums had oddball collections that used to be someone's hobby—like the Burl's now-stolen butterflies. This museum was just odder than most.

The small parking lot was full, so he wandered through nearby streets until he found a place with an empty meter. Several quarters later, he had enough time to talk with Chuck for an hour and a half.

Joe walked briskly in case it started to rain again. Being at the museum, though, made him smile in spite of himself. An old school bus balanced precariously over the top of the former shoe factory building, while a giant praying mantis watched a four-story Ferris wheel. A handful of preschoolers and their parents ignored the half-airplane stuck in the wall above them and tossed plastic balls at each other in a netted McDonald's-like play yard.

And that was just on the outside.

Joe shook his head. The last time he'd been to the museum was to usher one of Teri's nephews through, and the ornery kid had purposely ditched him in the crystal and mirrors cave room. He'd finally found him in the crawl-through spaces that used to be the shoe conveyer belts. Talk about claustrophobic! Although it was a featured area of the museum, it certainly wasn't made for adults. And then he'd lost a shoe on the long slide that ran from the top floor to the first.

Joe paid his admission and then checked his phone. Reliable as always, Chuck had left another text with very specific instructions: *Take elevator to 3rd floor, go left at the boxing robot, through the Western bar to Insect Room.*

He passed the entrance to Beatnik Bob's, a carnival midway exhibit, and ducked through the massive red curtain that closed off the Western bar and party room.

Here, at last, a bit of normalcy. Besides himself, there were only a young man and woman at the far end of the room, chatting with a museum employee. He overheard "reception" and "wedding cake" and decided that they must be thinking about renting out the huge, bare industrial room. To him, it had all the appeal of an abandoned warehouse, but he supposed that tables and chairs and mingling guests would might it feel more festive. He slipped into the adjoining Western bar and crossed the wood dance floor. This part looked like a party room, for sure, he thought. Just past the dance floor, he found the Insect Room and entered.

He looked at his phone: 9:07.

It was a fairly small room but contained mounted specimens of both colorful and crawly insects in a floor-to-ceiling and wall-to-wall display. Joe spotted several butterflies and grimaced. He'd had enough of those.

Three minutes later, Chuck entered the room, right on time, clutching a paper folio. Joe raised his eyebrows and tried not to laugh. Chuck was wearing a full clown suit, complete with red hair, nose, and huge shoes.

"Chuck," Joe said slowly, unable to contain his grin, "was it really necessary to meet me wearing a disguise?"

Chuck's mouth turned down, in spite of the red painted smile around it. "It's not a disguise. I'm moonlighting as a character in Beatnik Bob's circus room."

"Moonlighting?"

"Well, Dressor doesn't exactly pay very well."

Joe couldn't help it. He laughed. "No argument from me, but I gotta tell you, you look ridiculous."

Chuck put on a forced happy face. "But I make the kids laugh and the people here like me. And they pay on time."

"Whatever works, bro."

Chuck shrugged. "I don't have much time. There's a class of third graders coming in about twenty minutes."

"OK," Joe said, pointing to the folio. "Let's have a look."

Chuck nodded. "I checked for Bea's last cases." He paused. "I assume one of her relatives had some questions about her death?"

Joe took a moment to consider his answer. "Yes, well, I'm not going to divulge the exact person, but they needed some reassurance that it was just an accident. I guess they've watched too many TV cop shows, but I said I'd look into it."

Chuck nodded, his clown hair flopping. "Yeah, I've discovered there's a certain amount of hand-holding in this profession." He gave Joe a list.

Joe scanned it quickly. "It seems to be missing a few—the Burl case, for instance, with the missing butterfly collection."

Chuck sidled next to him, bumping him with his big shoes. "Sorry!" He looked over his shoulder. "No, that's all that was in the files."

"Strange," Joe murmured. He wondered what else was missing.

Chuck produced more papers. "You also asked about Smitters Automotive. They got regular payments, some of them large for a car inspection." He squinted through face paint. "Did you guys do a lot of stolen or repo auto cases? I've only seen one or two in the time I've been there."

"No, we didn't," Joe said, frowning. "What else do you have?"

"I looked up Floyd Chapin, the guy involved with your current case? He used to work as an auto mechanic before turning to crime."

"Interesting. Do you know where he worked?"

"Several places. Smitters was one of them."

Chuck shuffled the stack together. "And I tailed Dressor's lady myself, by accident. They were eating dinner at a place I went to get carry-out."

Joe shook his head. "It's hard to say it's an affair when all they do is eat together. It could be some kind of business deal, or a client he's taking care of by himself."

"Yeah, I'm trying to calm my mom about it. She's not convinced." Chuck looked up as a few kids started coming in. "I took a couple of pix. They're in here, too, along with some background info on the Lotus Moon store."

"Thanks! Hey, I really appreciate your help."

"You're welcome. Let me know if you find out anything else about that woman. Now, I gotta get going. I can hear the kids."

"Wait—what's the best way out of here?"

Chuck leaned his head slightly to the left. "This way."

Joe followed Chuck through the hall with broken St. Louis architectural details and around to the miniature Circus room, complete with child-size benches and a small performance area. A busload of school kids were being ushered in by their teacher and parent helpers.

Chuck stopped and waved to the kids, who

started yelling and clapping. "Keep going to your left," he said to Joe over the din. "You'll find the elevator or the stairs, they're both that direction." He grabbed a noise-maker and turned to the crowd. "Yuck, yuckity, yuck! I'm Clown Clowny Chuck!" He then squeezed the bulb on his horn several times, aiming it all around the room.

Joe shook his head. Actually, Chuck was pretty good, as clowns go. He slipped out and found the stairs, stopping at the second floor snack bar. He ordered a Coke and sat down at a small table in a quiet corner, then started leafing through the thick stack that Chuck had given him. Apparently his friend had checked several kinds of records, including a few that Joe didn't have access to anymore.

The guy was thorough—he had to give him that.

Joe studied a few photocopies. So, the owner of the Lotus Moon was Strawberry Moon, and she'd been in business for several years according to tax and incorporation records. Chuck had also included a birth record showing she was the daughter of Cassidy Blue and Lotus Moon, both now deceased.

Good hippie names, Joe thought, remembering his conversation with the saleslady there.

He picked up the photos Chuck had taken. Dressor, with a cat-grin look on his face—ugh. And the woman, reaching for his hand. Or the salt. It was hard to tell.

Joe stared at the photo. There, on the back of her left hand, was a tattoo.

Of a strawberry. Just like her name.

Just like fired mechanic Hector Gonzales had told him about.

Holy crap!

Chapter 15

The door to the garage creaked open and shut. Joe looked up from his place at the kitchen table and quickly swept Chuck's papers under a magazine.

Teri—or Bea—came in with a few bags of groceries.

"Hi, hon," Joe said cautiously. "How's your day?"

She raised one eyebrow, very Bea-like. "Long lines everywhere. And she keeps picking out all this healthy crap." She set her bags down on the counter. "When I cook, I never can find something decent to eat."

It was Bea, then.

She sighed and started unpacking the bags. "Have you found out anything new about my case?"

"Not really," he lied. "Chuck gave me some financial records and stuff like that. Nothing definitive. I'm gonna have to study them."

Bea gave him a sharp look. "I see. Maybe I can help you when I'm done here." She opened a cupboard and put away some granola and whole wheat flour. "By the way, I'm sorry I made you sleep in the living room last night."

Joe shrugged. "I'm sure it was better for both of us." It was becoming much harder to stay out of trouble these days. It seemed all he did was piss off one or the other of the women, sometimes both.

Bea sat down opposite him at the table, a bit too close to the pile he'd stashed under the magazine. "Joe, I just wanted to tell you, I really appreciate all the work you've done to uncover my murderer. Even if you never find him or her."

"Thanks for saying that. This hasn't been easy."

"I know. I shouldn't have gotten you involved. I've caused you—and Teri—a bucket-load of problems that you didn't ask for. And I really shouldn't have—" She paused. "You know. Involved you that other way."

Joe shook his head. "We shouldn't have—"

"Well," Bea said slowly, "what's done is done."

"Yeah." It'd be nice if it were possible to turn back time and make different decisions. But, if given the chance, would he make even a bigger mess of it? He sighed. "You know, I really would like to finish your case so you could—" Joe stopped. How could he put it nicely? Leave to the great hereafter and let him return to his own life? Quit making him feel like a cheater every time she so much as talked to him?

Maybe his guilt was getting to him.

"Rest in peace?" Bea looked sad and serious this morning, a very unusual combination for her. "When the accident happened, I saw a light in the distance, just like the stories say. But I couldn't get there."

"A light? Really?"

"It was beautiful. Alive, somehow." She sighed. "I couldn't move because I was held back. I was supposed to fix something in my life, and I didn't do it. Maybe I'll never get to that light," she said, a little shake in her voice. "I think I'm running out of time."

"Don't give up yet," Joe said. "We'll figure it out."

She nodded, then stood up suddenly. "Figure what out? Oh, damn! How'd I get here?"

Teri. Their transitions were becoming as fast as a light switch, and pretty hard to keep up with. Joe suppressed a groan. He hurried to her side and put an arm around her. "You just got home. Maybe you're just feeling a little lightheaded." He led her to the living room and sat her down in the armchair. "Better?"

Teri put her elbows on the arms of the chair and leaned back. "I sorta remember driving. No, I do remember driving home. And the garage door going up." She paused and peered at him. "And then, I remember talking to you about something, but I don't know what it was."

Bea had warned him about Teri becoming more aware of her. He smiled weakly. "We were talking about you going to the grocery store."

Teri looked down for a moment. "Yeah, yeah, I was there. For some reason, I keep wanting to pick up junk food. I've never wanted junk food before."

"Maybe it's a craving of some kind."

She shrugged one shoulder. "I guess." She gave him a stern look. "I better not be pregnant."

It was Joe's turn to shrug. "Well, we'll deal with it if you are. I'd guess you're just tired."

She leaned back again and closed her eyes. "This—whatever I have—is driving me crazy. Did I tell you the doctor ordered an MRI of my brain?"

"Besides all the blood tests you had earlier? Did they find anything?"

"Not yet. All the tests have come back normal. Except I keep losing parts of my day." Teri opened her eyes. "Lately, though, it's like I can almost remember."

Joe cleared his throat. "Hey, listen, I had an early appointment today and I didn't have time to shave. So, why don't I get cleaned up and then make lunch? You can rest in the meantime."

She picked up a sofa pillow and tucked it behind her head. "Thanks, that'd be nice."

Joe ran up the stairs to the master bathroom. Damn! Why did things always have to be so complicated? And why did it all depend on him? He took off his shirt and grabbed the can of shaving foam. Well, he at least could look half-way decent even if he wasn't finding any answers.

He tried not to cut himself. It was hard to keep his mind on what he was doing. Three different cases—the Burls, Bea, and Dressor—all crashing together. Was it a strange and cosmic coincidence?

Yeah, with a ghost involved? Probably not.

He finished shaving, splashed on some cologne and put his shirt back on. Joe called out as he descended the stairs. "So, what would you like for lunch? A BLT? Grilled cheese? Those are my specialties, you know."

There was no answer.

Joe scanned the living room. It was empty.

He walked into the kitchen. "Hon?" But Teri wasn't in there either.

Then he saw the mess on the table. The magazine had been moved and Chuck's photos were spread out. There, front and center, was the close-up shot of the strawberry tattoo.

Oh, shit!

Joe ran to the garage. The light was still on but

Teri's car was gone. He grabbed his keys and wallet and buzzed the garage door open. Bea must have come back and remembered how the tattoo connected to her case. She'd want answers, and she was not one to back down until she got them. Even if it proved dangerous.

A sudden thought struck him—surely not! But he bolted inside again and up the steps to the guest room, where the gun safe was kept.

The closet door was wide open, and so was the safe. Joe swore and ran back downstairs again, trying not to panic.

One of the pistols was missing.

&⳿Ↄ⳿Ꙩ

Joe sped onto highway 270 and then ramped onto I-70 West. He'd made several calls on his cell and Teri hadn't answered any of them. His right foot pressed harder on the accelerator. He was probably driving too fast but he didn't really care.

Once he hit the town limits in St. Charles, though, Joe slowed down. What on earth was he going to do? If Teri—that is, Bea—were already in the Lotus Moon and arguing or threatening Strawberry Moon, how was he going to stop it?

Get a grip, man! He'd think of something.

The streets were quiet except for a few shoppers. He eased into the Lotus Moon parking lot, half-expecting to see dead bodies, but the only thing there was the owner's BMW, parked close to the back door, like before.

He tapped the steering wheel with his ring. Something wasn't right. He turned around and drove back to the street. Maybe Bea parked Teri's VW somewhere close and walked.

Joe scanned the street, but there was no sign of the car. A quick tour of several nearby blocks yielded the same negative result.

Where in the hell was she?

Joe returned to the Lotus Moon parking lot and got out of the car. A sick feeling hit the pit of his stomach. Bea had torn out of the house, probably angry, and she had a weapon—not a good combination.

Car or no, he'd have to go and look for her in the store.

Joe stared at the grinning moon lamps in the front window, then pushed the door with the moon-chime and went in.

No one was in the front of the store. How odd!

He reminded himself that St. Charles was a small town and didn't have the crime problems of St. Louis, but to leave the store unattended didn't seem very smart.

Unless they were attending to something in the back—like a madwoman with a gun.

He hovered near the back entry and listened. Two people seemed to be arguing, a man and a woman, but he couldn't make out what they were saying. He slipped down the dim corridor toward the voices, but they fell silent. He turned a corner and found a doorway opening into a large, unlit warehouse room. He paused by the door, keeping to the shadows.

The room was stacked with yet more merchandise, which was unusual for a store this size. From Teri's workplaces, Joe knew that most stores wanted their goods out and on display to get them sold faster. And the goods here were of a different quality than what was out front. There were furniture pieces with turnings and fancy wood grains, finely-painted vases, expensive-looking marble and gilt statues, and other items that could have come from houses like the Burls'.

Maybe they did, he thought.

Joe crept into the room to get a better look. Here and there was a jewelry box or humidor, figurines, tea sets, crystal lamps and half-packed chandeliers. Top-notch stuff, all of it.

The voices started up again, along with close-sounding footfalls. "Look, we had a deal," the woman said.

"Yes, we did," a very gravelly and familiar voice said. "And you get your cut and no more."

Before Joe could find something to hide behind, the lights went on.

There, with one hand on the light switch and cash in the other, stood Strawberry Moon, with Donald Dressor right behind her.

Chapter 16

Strawberry let out a short scream.

"What the fuck?" Dressor passed his money to Strawberry and swiftly reached for his holster. "Shurjack?"

Joe soon found himself staring into the barrel of Dressor's pistol. His mouth went dry and he couldn't say a word.

Dressor took off the safety. "Hands where I can see them!"

Joe raised his hands carefully, watching his former boss' every move.

"I thought someone had been snooping into my affairs." Dressor waved the gun menacingly. "A lot of my files were moved around. How'd you get in the office? I had the locks changed."

Joe wasn't about to tell him Chuck had done the snooping for him. "Um, what's with the gun, Dressor? I just came back here because nobody was up front."

Strawberry stuffed the cash into a nearby humidor. She gave him a dubious look.

"Shut up! Do you take me for a fool? Strawberry

said someone had tailed her in the park the other day. I should've known it was you."

"I don't have a clue what you're talking about," Joe said, trying to be convincing. He'd seen Dressor mad before, but this was different. His eyes were glazed over, chilled and unreasonable.

A hard thought hit him. *I'm going to die.*

Dressor looked down his nose at him. "Don't have a clue. Right. This is really unfortunate, Shurjack. I told you that you weren't cut out to be a P.I."

The front door chime tinkled faintly.

Strawberry looked at Dressor. "I'll go take care of whoever that is. You take care of things here." She left.

Dressor seemed to enjoy being the heavy. "Just you and me, Shur-jerk. Move it! We're taking this discussion into another room where none of the merchandise gets broken."

Joe felt his mouth fall open. His life was about to be over, and all Dressor could think of was his freakin' pilfered goods?

"I said, move it, Shurjack!"

"So," Joe said, taking a small step and trying to stall, "aren't you going to tell me what this is all about?"

Dressor gave an ugly laugh. "This ain't the movies, son. I don't have to tell you shit." He swung around behind Joe and pushed the gun barrel into his back. "You've seen something you shouldn't have. Much like your friend, Bea. Good enough for you? Now, move!"

Before they got more than two steps, something hit the other side of the wall. Dressor froze and pulled Joe to a halt. "What the hell?"

"Where are you, Joe, you son of a bitch!" It was Teri, somewhere out in the hall.

Joe needed to warn her! "Te—!"

"Shh!" Dressor warned, the gun still in Joe's back.

"You fucking son-of-a-bitch! You slept with her— and used my body! How could you!" she screamed, nearly into view now. "We hate you! Both of us!"

We? Oh, no!

"What?" Dressor eased the gun slightly and snorted. "This nutcase is after you?" he whispered.

Then Joe saw a flash of her in the darkened doorway, gun drawn. The look on her face stopped him cold. Her eyes sparked and her face was flushed. He instantly knew she wasn't there to save him.

No, he was really going to die!

Dressor spun Joe into him for cover and drew up his pistol.

But he wasn't quick enough. Teri fired first.

A too-close rush of air whistled past Joe. Dressor

screamed and fell back.

Joe gasped, but Teri's attention was completely on his old boss. Joe turned and saw that Dressor's shoulder was now a brilliant red. His shooting hand was now useless, and his gun clattered to the floor.

Joe touched the side of his own head and felt nothing but a little sweat. A lot of sweat, actually.

Teri pushed past him and grabbed a lamp, smashing it. She ripped the cord from the base. "Here!" she said. "Tie him up."

Joe stared at her, uncomprehending.

Dressor started to swat at her with his good arm, but she raised her gun again. "Don't try anything. I can't miss at this range." She kicked at his feet. "Sit down and face the wall." She turned toward Joe. "Come on, Joe, tie him up."

Dressor groaned but sat as ordered. Joe gathered his wits and quickly grabbed the older man's wrists, securing them with the lamp cord. Some of Dressor's blood got on his sleeve.

Teri still held the gun on Dressor. "OK," she said to Joe. "Now get out your cell and call 911. Tell them to bring an ambulance, too."

She was eerily calm. Joe called and gave what details he could. Everything seemed surreal. The operator was excruciatingly thorough and kept him on the line for several minutes. As soon as he hung up, two cops burst into the room. One had muscles that barely fit into his shirt.

"St. Charles Police!" the other one called.

"Standing down," Teri announced, putting her gun down and her hands up.

Joe raised his hands, also. The thinner cop, weapon drawn, rushed to examine Dressor.

"Teri? Teri Matthews?" the muscular one asked.

She blinked. "Brad Legault? From high school?"

"It is you!" Brad said. "Wow, it's been a while!"

"Officer Legault? Crime scene, remember?" the other officer said, not kindly. He also called for an ambulance with his shoulder mike. "One man down, shot in right shoulder. One woman down, age about forty, possible concussion."

Joe shuddered. It had to be Strawberry Moon. That would explain the thud they'd heard.

"Right, sorry. Guess we'll have to catch up later." Brad straightened into a more official pose. "Everyone has to go in for questioning," he announced. He looked at Teri. "And since you had the gun, I will have to cuff you."

"Sure," she said, sounding almost eager.

Joe stared in disbelief. Was this the same woman who burst in here and nearly killed him?

A siren sounded and the place filled with people. The officers secured the scene while EMT's got Dressor into an ambulance. Brad led Joe and Teri outside to a mass of cars with red and blue blinking lights. More police had arrived, as well as many onlookers. Strawberry leaned on a police car, with an ice pack on her head. Brad started to separate Joe and Teri when Joe stopped him.

"I just need a minute," Joe said quietly.

"OK by me," Brad said, then walked off a short distance to confer with other officers.

Joe looked at Teri, her hands cuffed behind her. "I thought you were going to kill me."

"Look, Joe, if I'd wanted you dead, we wouldn't be having this conversation."

Joe blinked. "Then—you're not really mad?"

"Oh, no, baby," she said, a little fire coming into her voice. "I'm beyond mad. You cheated on me, Joe! Bea told me—or rather, I learned it when we merged. How could you?"

There was no good answer, Joe knew. "I messed up. I never wanted to hurt you."

"Right." She looked away from him.

"Um, where did you go? I thought you'd get here way before me."

Teri's mouth turned down. "I should have. Bea

got us lost."

Joe reached out and touched her arm, but she shook him off. He swallowed hard. "We'll talk soon."

She glared at him. "Don't count on it."

Big Brad came back. "Time to go to the station. This way, Teri. Mr. Shurjack, you go with Officer Jamison, there."

"I'll need to call my dad. He knows a good lawyer," Teri said as Brad put his paws on her, helping her into the car.

Yeah, Joe thought. He knew a lawyer, too.

Chapter 17

Joe cradled the landline receiver between his shoulder and ear. "Hey, Joshua! Good to hear from you, too." He sat down on his worn sofa. "Yeah, I got your check. Thanks."

The lawyer chuckled. "This case turned out to be quite something, eh? We started with butterflies and uncovered a backdoor fencing operation. The D.A.'s office found some very interesting emails that had been erased from Ms. Moon's computer."

"Really?" Joe made a mental note to learn how to do that. "Such as?"

"Correspondence to various black markets, making inquiries as to their interest in her newly-acquired wares. According to your man Chuck, several of her items included lost property cases that had come through Dressor's office."

"Wow. Pretty damning."

"I'll say. I'm glad I'm not representing him! Can't sing or dance that well."

"Have you heard how it's going in the courts?" Joe asked, readjusting his hold on the phone. It'd only been a couple of months and he knew it took time, but he was curious.

"Well, according to my sources, Ms. Moon didn't say a word. But her assistant, Emily Hartsberg, ratted her out—please pardon the cliché. Even mentioned the murder of Floyd Chapin, especially since she could plea-bargain to a lesser sentence."

"Was he killed because of the botched burglary?" Joe asked.

"Yes. Apparently Ramina Burl's death wasn't planned. She hired him herself, did you know that? There was also an email that flat out told Ramina that the collection was the museum's, so she damn well knew she couldn't sell it to anyone legitimate."

"Yeah, that's what I thought she knew."

"Clever thinking on your part," Joshua said. "There's more, if you want to hear it."

"Please."

"Well, Ms. Moon recommended Chapin to steal and fence the butterfly collection—which, as you know, he did a lousy job of—but Ramina surprised him that night in the billiards room. He had a gun and shot without thinking. Dressor didn't take kindly to this faux pas, especially since he didn't get much money out of the goods, so had Smitters make it look like Chapin drowned."

Joe shuddered. "That's pretty vicious. I can't believe I worked two years for that guy."

"Well, be happy that you didn't feel any more wrath than getting fired," Joshua said. "He wasn't all that smart this time, though, in covering his tracks. Seems like cleaning up can make a bigger mess sometimes."

Joe thought about Bea and Teri and silently agreed.

"Smitters, who is also plea-bargaining, admitted to tampering with Bea's car. Dressor paid him for that. According to papers taken from Dressor's office, she must have discovered part of the earlier illegal goings-on. As I said, Chuck has been most helpful in finding evidence. And with the additional information you've provided, I expect Dressor will have a hard time defending much of anything."

"Good to hear," Joe said, half-heartedly.

"So we've managed to take out a whole ring of crooks, making it safer for the good citizens of Metropolis."

"Thanks, Joshua, but I don't feel much like Superman."

Joshua lowered his voice. "Any news of your wife?"

"My soon-to-be ex? She's staying with her brother

for now. She said she'd come by later this afternoon."

Joshua was quiet for a moment. "Listen, Joe, you did a great job for me, and I don't forget people who do great jobs. If you'd like me to take a look at the papers for you—"

"No need. We didn't have much, so there isn't much to argue about. Thanks, anyway."

"Well, the offer stands. And I may have another case for you soon. I'm waiting to hear if they wish to retain me as their attorney."

Joe reached for his beer with his free hand. "Thanks for that, too. I've gotten some work from Chuck and a couple of referrals, so I'm keeping busy." He took a generous gulp.

"We'll keep in touch," Joshua said, and hung up after good-byes.

Joe looked down at his half-eaten sandwich on the coffee table. Teri had taken the kitchen set, most of the dishes and pots and pans, their bedroom set, and a few other pieces, along with her car. She hadn't been a jerk about it, but it had left him with a substandard household. Not that it mattered much, since they had to sell the house, too.

He finished his sandwich and beer and cleaned up a little. The doorbell rang, and he went to open the door. It was Teri, right on time. She wore jeans and a tee, with a tight little buttoned sweater on top. It was very casual but it was definitely her, not Bea.

"Hi," he said softly.

She shrugged one shoulder. "Hi, yourself. You doing OK?"

"Yeah. You?"

"Pretty good, actually." She walked into the living room with a more confident stride than usual and sat on the lone chair beside the sofa. "I'm moving in two weeks."

Joe frowned. "Where to?"

"New Mexico, of all places. Brad told me about some law enforcement openings in Bernalillo County, so I signed up for the training academy. He said with my shooting skills, I'd be a natural. He's checking it out, too. We're both tired of the Midwest winters and all the tornados the rest of the year."

Officer Brad, again. "You seeing a lot of him?" Joe asked, then wished he hadn't said anything.

She cocked her head slightly. "Yeah, I am."

A silence fell between them. Teri spoke first. "So, you got the papers, right? Have you signed them?"

Joe shuffled the stack on one end of the coffee table and produced the document. "Yeah, I got them." He picked up a pen and toyed with it. "Teri, I want you to know a few things. I really thought it was you in that Albuquerque motel. It felt like the time when we first got married."

She pursed her lips. "And in our bedroom later? And in Bea's apartment earlier?"

"I can't say the same for the night here." Joe looked down. "And we were very drunk the night we were at her apartment. I don't remember what happened and she never told me."

"Well, she told me—or rather, I found out from her memories when we were linked." Teri sniffed. "You want to know what happened? Not a lot, other than some groping and undressing. You both passed out before going all the way." She looked at him sternly. "Not that it makes a difference. In my mind, the intent was there. That's as much cheating on me as what you did later."

"Teri, it was all a huge mistake. I never set out to do that or to hurt you. Please believe me."

She shrugged again. "Yeah, that's what she said, too. I'm not sure I believe either one of you, but it's nice to hear it, at least."

Joe laid the pen on the table. "By the way, has she bothered you? Is she—gone?"

Teri looked thoughtful for a moment. "Am I still possessed? No, I'm not. She left right after we shot Dressor. She was a bit hard to control at that point.

She really wanted to do him in. I had to push her out to keep a steady hand on the trigger. She never came back. I assume she went where she wanted to go, thank God."

At least he'd been able to help find her murderer. Correction, murderers. Bea should have resolved her issues, then, and could be at rest now. He looked at Teri. "Are you feeling OK now, no more blackouts?"

She shook her head. "No. I'm just fine. Better than fine. My depression's gone, too." She looked him straight in the eye. "Look, Joe, I appreciate your interest, but we need to finish our business here. You know as well as I do that we just weren't any good together. I wasn't happy, you weren't happy—that's not a good way to run a marriage."

He looked down. "I know, you're right. I just hate to end things this way." He raised his head. "As long as you're yourself again."

"I am, with no after-effects." She tapped the papers. "Sign, please? That's what I came over for."

He grimaced and took the pen and scratched his name on the various places her lawyer had highlighted. He handed the stack to her. "The realtor said the house should sell reasonably fast, but you know there isn't much equity in it. I'll be glad to send your half as soon as it closes."

"We already split the bank account. I don't need any more money right now. My dad's going to help me with my move, and my brother's throwing in some, too."

"That's good." Joe heaved a sigh. "I'm also glad they didn't come over here and shoot me."

"Oh," Teri said a little too brightly, "they never really liked you, so they were glad we split."

"Great," Joe said, almost under his breath.

"Sorry. I probably shouldn't have told you that."

Joe shook his head. "At least I don't have to look over my shoulder for them."

"Yeah, don't worry about that." She stood up. "I'll send you my new address after I get settled in Albuquerque. For now, I'll be staying with a friend of Brad's who lives there."

At least it wasn't Brad himself. Joe chided himself for the twinge of jealousy. She was a free woman, now, and could go and do whatever she wanted, see whomever she wanted. She'd acquired a new-found confidence somehow, and it suited her.

He sighed. It was good to see her doing well, even if it was sad at the same time.

Joe walked her to the door. New Mexico had seemed like an interesting place. Maybe he'd have to take a trip there again when he had some free time.

Maybe they could have a beer together and reminisce about old times. In spite of what she said, they'd had some good times. At least, they'd been good for him.

"Oh, get that, will you? Tell my brother I'm running about a half-hour late."

Joe frowned. "Huh?"

"Bye, Joe." She kissed him on the cheek and left.

What was that all about? Before he could wonder very long, the landline rang. Joe walked over and saw the caller ID. It was her brother, just as she'd said.

A chill ran over him as he reached for the receiver.

No after-effects, he told himself.

Of course not.

About the author:

L. Phillips Carlson has more than 130 published articles, short stories and poems to her credit, most under a different pen name. She also worked as a copy editor for a group of nationally-distributed magazines, wrote and edited a local newsletter for a decade, and penned an award-winning church history. When not writing, Ms. Carlson travels widely, sings in a symphonic chorus, and tends to various members of her family. She lives in sunny New Mexico with her retired-engineer husband in a pueblo-style home they designed themselves.

For additional titles, please check the following:

Website

www.lphillipscarlson.com

Author page

www.amazon.com/author/lphillipscarlson